Double Dare
A Funny Fearless Friendship

RYCJ

Published by
OSAAT Entertainment

OSAAT Entertainment
P.O. Box 1057
Bryn Mawr, Pennsylvania, 19010-7057
www.osaatent.com

All rights reserved.

No part of this book may be reproduced or transmitted in any form or by any means, graphic, electronic, or mechanical, including photocopying, recording, taping, or by any information storage retrieval system, without the written permission of the publisher.

Second Edition.

Email the Author: rycj@osaatent.com

Copyright © 2015 RYCJ, Double dare. Fiction
Cover Design by Sunny Tellone

Library of Congress Control Number: 2015941532

ISBN: 978-0-9886907-0-7

Printed in the United States of America

Double Dare
A Funny Fearless Friendship

Chapter 1

Phyllis was a good woman. She didn't smoke. Didn't drink. Well, that is she didn't drink anything stronger than champagne, or its equivalent. She didn't swear. Didn't lie. Wouldn't cheat. Didn't gossip. Phyllis didn't do any of the things associated with bad. She basically, according to Mona, her best friend, didn't live.

Not that Mona was a bad person either, because she wasn't. But Mona considered herself a risk-taker. Those enjoying the journey, instead of going along for the ride—more like hanging on to the ride, letting it bounce and pounce them around…until they fell off.

But be it as it was, Phyllis married a man about as agnostic to her goodness as church was to a stripper club. He wasn't a real bad guy either, which that said, Phyllis didn't go to church either—due to the man she married, but…but… she did believe goodness ruled. She believed goodness excluded her from having to deal with a bumpy journey, and would somehow lead into a smooth satisfying life.

Didn't happen. She married Joe Witherspoon, a fun guy. A laugh-a-lot guy. Boastful. Braggart. Loud. Vulgar. Arrogant. A pushover sometimes. A bully all the time. Cursed. Swore. Drank. Marginally intelligent. By the scripture ignorant. And sssh…Joe chased women too.

But…but… he did consent to Phyllis working in the home. So give Joe one big brownie point. That one he believed in big time. His wife should not work outside the home, even if his chief reason for believing this had more to do with not wanting their paths to rear-end each other, traversing the same strip. People talked. Sooner or later, had Phyllis been out there working, she would have found out where Joe hung out after work and may have not been so good after that. Whether she joined him, or kicked him to the curb, her goodness resume would have been forever scarred.

This intro is important because this is how it all got started. This is how, and why, it all happened.

For Joe's fortieth birthday Phyllis decided she was going to throw her husband a birthday bash. Why not? He deserved it. He deserved to be rewarded for being a supportive and fun-loving husband and father. Plus Joe had added a deck onto the house, which was another thing Joe was. He was the biggest showoff of all times. Any occasion he could think to celebrate, he'd invite over his colorful friends, none who had as much as he had of course, and brag all night long while Phyllis busied herself making sure all the proper essentials were clean and available to help Joe along in his knack for showing off.

Basically what this meant was Phyllis was skilled at making sure the drapes, carpet, upholstery, and other household essentials matched. Keeping those vacuum lines fresh. Ensuring the right utensils went with the right dish. If Joe were expecting 50 guests, she'd make sure there was enough to feed 100 people. And that everyone Joe invited over was happy. So then why on earth would Phyllis do what she did?

She called Mona, her good friend of many years, and together they planned an all-out bash for Joe. Well, they didn't plan this thing together together. Mona wasn't quite like Phyllis in the believing department. She did not believe Phyllis should surprise Joe with a formal affair. This was not Joe's style. Why would she ever think it was belabored good's definition?

"Maybe you should tone it down a little," Mona warned, "you know how Joe is."

Joe wasn't a formal type guy, and really neither was Phyllis. She may have buddied up with the elite while Joe worked his important high-tech job at an IT security-based company, but she really was a casual woman who just so happened to marry a man who bought a home in the hills and thought he was it. They weren't it. At least not that type of it.

Forget formal attire, Joe was a bandline and khakis type guy. Weekends he wore Jordans, and baseball caps backward. He also wore his jeans a little baggy, and swore it was cool to wear shades 11 at night… thinking no one would know he had a little more than too much to drink. How Phyllis thought this type of guy should mix and mingle with the elite was beyond wise inspection.

But this was Phyllis's thing. She read and loved all the fairy tale classics; Snow White, Cinderella, and even Harry Potter, with the resplendent castles carved into the story, and as such always dreamed of the day when she'd get to throw a ball of her own. So who was Mona to knock down her dream? This sounded close to living. It certainly could be called daring…which Mona was no splice when it came to daring—hence, the real story on its way.

The big day came and a handful of people Phyllis associated with while Joe worked and…cough…flirted, filtered into their lush almost…gag…estate. They didn't know much about Joe, being new to the neighborhood, how Phyllis snookered them in to attending in the first place, but believed a woman as good as Phyllis, and as expert in her homemaking skills, would naturally be married to a man just as cultured.

Mona met the elite at the door, for she was the hostess. Politely, as tuxedos and gowns glided by, she collected minks and stoles and pointed the elite to the lovely deck Phyllis had all decked out in the splendors of fine dining and living.

About thirty minutes into drinks, d'oeuvres, and light banter; with just about all guests accounted for, Mona rushed upstairs to see what was holding Phyllis and Joe up. She had a pretty good idea what it was, but to be sure she sprinted up the Steeplechase staircase to confirm what she already knew.

They were in the room at each other's throats arguing about this ostentatious affair. Yes! Joe of all people was all swelled up around the collar about Phyllis surprising him with a party that was by all means outside his league. He couldn't brag to those stiffs downstairs. Was Phyllis out of her caviar mind!?!

The surprise, a surprise no more, Joe bittered up even more when he realized he was required to wear a tux. Yes!

Phyllis had done the daring. Neatly laid out on the bed was a pale sea blue tux affixed to a royal blue satin cummerbund.

When Mona saw the tux and heard Joe's cries, "I wouldn't dare wear that!?!" it was all she could do not to break out laughing.

Using some of her negotiating skills, Mona calmed the worked up Joe down. The night so young had so much time left to see this daring feat play out. Mona could get like this. She rarely passed up a chance to laugh. And not that she wanted to see either Phyllis, or Joe hurt, but really? Had she been able to convince Phyllis into hosting an affair Joe might like, then Phyllis would be disappointed, even if the affair turned out like it always did when she was the host.

Fair was fair. Phyllis wanted to do the party her way, and Mona wasn't stopping her. At least she could be credited for getting Joe to partly go along…albeit, dressed in jeans, a leather vest, a fly silk shirt, and a suede tam. But when the swanky met the swan, the hilarity dial shot up humor thermometer.

The expressions registering on each guest's face as Phyllis introduced them to Joe stretched the word laughter the span of two or three glossaries. Those people were some kind of repulsed; so repulsed that they left before the cake was cut. One woman took one disgusted look at Joe and immediately turned to her husband and fell into his chest, bawling like a baby. She couldn't even tell Phyllis why she had to leave. She left it up to her husband to sheepishly explain.

Most, however, remained polite and palely upbeat, leaving out one by one telling Phyllis one lie after the next for their hasty departure. But Phyllis didn't seem to mind too much, on account of seeing how happy Joe was…getting louder and louder every time another one left out the door.

Sad, and not the greatest story ever told about Joe, that story soon forthcoming…perhaps, but it was this event that started unraveling Phyllis.

Soon after she started getting dis-invites to socials she used to attend; the Women's Bridge Club…Book Club…Bible Study…Put-Put League…Tango Cabals, and related social activities. The dis-invite stated the group had disbanded, but thanked her for her participation and would contact her with any further updates. No one ever did, though Phyllis soon learned the ladies were gathering under different names.

Phyllis wised up after that. She put two and two together and came to one conclusion. It was Joe. She was being snubbed because of him. Had he worn the tux, and acted somewhat couth, it was possible none of this would've happened.

She turned really bitter about it, the makings for a perfect concoction for fun. It didn't exactly happen overnight though. The ride still needed a little more greasing, and oil first…

Chapter 2

Mona got in her ear. "You've got to live Phyl! He's living the life he wants, and so should you!"

She was tired of hearing it. The same day, each and every day, her fun always depended on this one's fun, or that one's fun, or his fun! Anyone's fun, but her fun. Phyllis wasn't living. She was just hanging on to a ride that was going to sooner or later, buck her off.

And not to harp all on Phyllis, she didn't have it all together either. She was married to Frank, not as bad as Joe, but another harper who sometimes tried to make her responsible for his fun.

Frank didn't care for her working at a run-down theatre that refused to close its doors, trying to stay in the town almanac as the oldest theatre in the country. So what she had moved up to managing the facility. Big deal. It in fact only made her more of an underachiever since less than a hundred people (a year) ever went to the theatre. And yeah, so what their visitors were majorly tourists who heard about the theatre in places as far away as Japan. She burned up more gas getting there in one day than she earned all year!

So while Phyllis cried about Joe, she wasn't happy about Frank either. Theatre was her dream. As a child she pined for the day when she might make it all the way to Broadway. She worked hard at it too, but had doors slammed in her face every time she reached for a script, starting with her first theatre teacher who told her she'd never make it because her eyes were too big.

Though her first theatre teacher's remark became a riddle too late solved, Phyllis wasn't the only one handing off the blame baton. Mona grabbed one too. Both of them needed to live a little, which Mona started working on the moment this picture came into view.

On the side of her meager theatre earnings, she started her own online business. In the first year she made a killing designing matrixes to match clients and services. She looped that killing into the stock market, and unbeknownst to Frank, made a killing there too.

That could be called living…somewhat. She never would've betted anyone she could make the money she ended up raking in, in that first year had she not stuck her neck out there and lived a little.

But then money wasn't everything. The excitement had worn off, and honestly…she started getting tired of hearing from clients greedier than she had been when she first got started. Not to blame any of them one bit. They hungered for money, and never tired of finding ways to rake it in, but that was it. That was their fun… their dream…what made their clock tick. She had another dream, and this wasn't it. Plus her back hurt sitting in a chair all day. And her neck hurt too. Saying nothing of the crinkles she started seeing creeping up around her eyes.

The straw that broke the camel's back was the day she and Phyllis spent all day looking for a recliner for Joe, this time an anniversary present. Like always, it had to be special, which nothing wrong there, except for them hanging on the opposite side of fun.

Mona told her, "girl, you're going through all of this trouble and Joe is probably going to tell you to take it back. It costs too much."

Joe was real particular about her spending. They really couldn't afford the house they lived in, and a whole lot of other things he splurged on trying to show out. So he checked up on her spending, to keep them from going overboard on her fun. Consequently Phyllis dressed a little homely, and developed this knack for knick-picking, being a pro at catching sales.

At any rate, she didn't believe Mona, and shopped till they almost dropped, finding a $3700 chair marked down to $700. It was a freaking steal! Even Mona was excited about this chair. It came with everything but the approval of Joe.

Mona was there. She witnessed Phyllis working the clerk, bargaining him down in $20 increments until the price reached the magic number available on her credit card. After that she then fussed with the same clerk to get the chair shipped on time, got it shipped on time, and Joe was mad as hell when he saw the charge to her account. Phyllis cried all week about that one incident. She tried to do something else nice for him and now this. Meanwhile, he had gone all out and bought her a gorgeous 18-karat bracelet, of course to show Frank up, who struggled to buy her decent bedroom slippers.

Phyllis cooed and cried all over the bracelet, tried to hang from a chandelier to thank him for it, and still was all torn up inside that he hadn't shown the same appreciation for the recliner she'd given him. Where was the fairness in it all?

So Mona told her. "Stop doing things for him and then blaming him for not being excited about it. He didn't want the chair. Damn! Was that so bad? You wanted the bracelet. Or did you? Darn it Phyllis, just make up your mind. What do you want? —How about we live a little!"

And then be darn it, Phyllis had just left her house, with the 18 karat bracelet jangling on her wrist and crying about Joe, which may have ended at another day of Joe Blues, had not Frank called and knocked the tail off the end of the day.

"So, what've you been doing all day baby," he asked like he asked no fewer than a zillion times before.

Irritated, as Phyllis had just left, she tersely replied, "work, as usual."

"You mean work like surfing the Net and emptying the frig don't you?"

It could've been a joke. In fact, it was a joke hardly meant to harm her, except it was no laughing matter. That mirror wasn't lying. Her behind was spreading faster than rotating tires spinning 175 mph sitting in a chair all day, even if she was exploding numbers that would blow his mind if he saw. The point was theatre had been her dream. Lorraine Hansberry was the image she sought to see, not a fat behind that was rich and nothing more.

Double Dare

Frank in effect told her to get up off her spreading duff and go after her fun. Sitting around raking in cash and blaming him for still being miserable wasn't going to change a thing. At best she'd spread further, and at worst it would make two miserable lots. Actually, make that four. She cheered Phyllis on the pity carnival, too.

All week she thought hard about what she could do. Ironically, acting or figuring her way on stage never entered the equation…at least not then. She reasonably concluded she had outgrown Hansberry. That's what happened when dreams were pushed aside to make money. You grow old, spread, and squash the dream.

But she could jump on a plane and fly to Africa. That occurred to her. It sounded reasonable. Maybe she could tie up the pilot and fly the plane herself. That certainly sounded adventurous, and fun, but…nah. She had better not even tease about doing something like that. The joke could end up on her, and not so funny.

Whatever she came up with had to be practical, at least starting out. And it had to be memorable. That meaning it had to be worth cashing in everything she owned moneywise to do it.

She must have preyed on it long enough because with very little warning she was telling Phyllis about a Broadway musical—Hairspray, and how inspirational it was that someone would come up with the theme, when Phyllis blurted, "I always wanted to see that! I tried to get Joe to take me, but you know how he is…" and she did her typical imitation of Joe when Joe didn't want to do something she wanted Joe to do.

"Wait..." Mona was online looking at show times. Why not? It was Saturday. The guys had plans to watch a game at a local sports bar that evening. It was a big championship game of sorts playing that night. They had just run out to buy these team spirit hats to rib any opponents they might later meet in the bar.

Imagine that, two forty-something year old grown men out buying silly hats to look sillier dressed in. But be it as it was, both she and Phyllis were fine with the silliness. They actually were happy the sports party would be taking place at the sports bar instead of in one of their homes. Instead of having to hear a room full of men shouting at the TV over the TV, spilling beer and dropping crumbs everywhere, this madness would be taking place somewhere else.

"There's a show showing at 3:15," Mona read off the screen. She looked at the computer clock, which showed 10:19am. "We can make that if..." and quickly she switched over to check the train schedule. The theatre was an hour train ride away. If they hurried they could catch the noon train, see the 3:15pm show, and be back on the train by 6ish or so, probably before their husbands even left home for the sports bar.

"Mo—but you're talking about going all the way up to the city? Maybe we should plan it instead of—"

"—Oh, come on Phyl! Why do we always gotta stick to these servant roles? What would you do if it was just you alone at home?"

Phyllis thought about it. What would she do? She didn't have a clue. She didn't have any kids at home anymore either. Just Joe. Old happy-go-lucky Joe who loved to laugh and have fun, and was actually enjoying what he loved to do. So, what was she afraid of?

"You know what? I'm on my way over!" Mona slammed down the phone, shoved herself into a pair of jeans, threw on a t-shirt she ripped down the front to jazz up her ample cleavage, grabbed a purse, and in almost one motion headed for her car. Didn't even leave a note. She figured they'd be back before their husbands returned home from the sports bar anyway.

Phyllis ran around the house too. She ran around the house looking for the number to the sports bar after calling Joe's cell phone and heard it ringing in the house. Too bad she didn't have Frank's cell phone number. She would've called him. But she wouldn't dare call Mona to ask for it. She'd ask why, and then jump on her for being such a worrywart.

Frantically searching the yellow pages did her no favors. The mall where she suspected they were was so new it wasn't listed yet. That was another thing about Phyllis. She was old-school. Right there in front of her was Joe's PC she only needed to turn on and fire up, but she never learned how to so much as turn the thing on. Just in the minutes she stood there before it, staring at it, Mona was out front laying on the horn. Yes, she was so desperate she was going to try and hunt down this number to have Joe paged in the mall if need be!

Hearing the horn made her heart thump, and her mouth feel a little sticky and dry. Joe sometimes left out of the house without telling her where he was going, or didn't always call to say why, or that he would be getting home from work late. But that was Joe. In the twenty-one years they had been married she never once left the house for a period longer than a few minutes without telling Joe where she was going, and when she would be back. It was just something she never did. Almost like how she never left the house without wearing underwear.

Oh, maybe that's what she'd do. Leave a note: Hey Joe, at the show with Mo! Love Phyl –

Chapter 3

"This is gonna be a day we're gonna remember!" Mona shrieked. "Girlfriend, we are going to have us some fun today!"

Mona peeled backwards as she was talking, her tires rolling over something lumpy both assumed was a curb, although the only curb was in front of them, the one she pulled up to, front forward.

After the car straightened up and Phyllis looked back did she realize what the lump was? Smokey, her neighbor's black cat.

"Oh no, Mo! Stop the car!" Phyllis cried.

"What? What's wrong?"

"It's Smokey. I think you ran over Smokey."

"Awl, he'll be alright," Mona said peering in the mirror and not seeing a cat back there.

"Mona, I don't think we should go. That's an omen right there, running over a black cat."

"Hush girl. It's foolish superstition. The only bad luck that'll be, and that's Smokey's, if it was him under my tires!"

Mona peeled out of the driveway forcing Phyllis to grab the door handle and press back in the seat. "Careful Mo—you could hit something and…"

...and Mona shoved on the gas pedal as hard as she could. "It's 11:09. Our train will be boarding in forty-five minutes!"

She barreled around a corner and flew onto the surface parking where a guardrail waited until she snatched the ticket out of the meter. The arm started to rise when, a little anxious, she tapped the gas, hitting the guardrail and bending the arm backwards. It made a begrudging crunching sound, but nothing that stopped Mona. It was now 11:42!

"Did you hear that," they both asked.

Mona looked back and saw the rail had managed to raise the rest of the way, so she figured it'd be okay. She parked and they hopped out of the car, and rushed for the train station.

"We'll just pay for our tickets on the train," Mona wheezed, huffing and running what she could assume was her fastest 50-yard dash ever.

"I didn't know they let you do that on these trains," Phyllis wheezed even louder, trailing Mona by a foot, 49-yards more to go.

As they ran, both sort of doubled over flailing their arms waving raggedy at a conductor checking for tickets by a gate. He waved back, letting them through, not wanting to hold these two up. They looked too desperate not to have tickets, figuring if he stopped them, they'd not only miss the train, but also probably pass out and die at his feet. Let them pass out on someone else's watch. He pulled the rope to seal the passageway from any other last minute passengers however.

With only a minute to spare, and on their last leg just as the conductor assumed, they both flew on the train, and collapsed into seats, the door sliding close seconds after they boarded.

An announcement came over the loudspeaker just as they were catching their breath, calling for tickets. 'Passengers, please sign your tickets and have them out for inspection, with a photo ID,' the robotic voice said.

"Whew, that was close," Mona huffed, just slightly less winded than Phyllis. "These train stations need to get a little bit better about situating the parking lot so far away from these trains. We could've had a massive heart attack and died."

"Tell me about it—"

"—Tickets please," a brassy voice hovered bitterly above them.

Mona looked up, still winded from the run. "Oh, sir, how much is the fare," she chugged out between puffs. "I'ma have to pay you in cash…or—" and she fumbled through her bag, briefly pausing to catch an irritated look. "You do accept major credit cards, right?"

"You don't have a ticket?" The conductor asked, not hiding the irritation in his voice either.

"No. I'll have to pay for our tickets now."

"Ma'am, we don't accept cash for fares on this train. We require tickets prior to boarding."

"I knew it," Phyllis scoffed, digging in her purse and looking around, forever the worrier about who might view her as uncivilized.

"Well, I did ask if you accepted major credit cards too," Mona said, in a nice crisper voice.

The conductor huffed and moved his mouth as if he was muttering, 'why you spoiled rotten old rich brats!'

But Mona didn't waste a second. At the time she didn't realize it, but she had a habit of acting out scenes she imagined. It was an old habit she picked up during her days of dreaming to become a Hansberry.

"Please sir, please. Me and my friend are trying to see a—" and she flipped the script mid-stream, just like that. "—for the love of Father God, please have mercy on us," she shrieked, doubling over to hold her face in her hands. "My son is in the hospital! I've got to see him! Please sir!"

That was one line she remembered well, but hated to use, especially when her son was small. She recalled a movie where someone did something similar, to end up accidentally hexing the person they lied on trying to get the upper hand. She couldn't remember the title of the movie, but never forgot the premise. Now that her son was grown however, maybe it wouldn't be so bad lying on his well-being.

Briskly the conductor walked away, into the next car without collecting other fares. Maybe he was going to call the police? Or how about stop the train and like the movie, 'Throw Mama from the Train,' throw them off the train, too.

Double Dare

A passenger on the opposite aisle leaned over to share a secret with Mona and Phyllis. "They don't like carrying cash on trains, but you can pay on the train. It'll just be more expensive," an elderly woman said.

And boy was it ever more expensive. A forty-eight dollar fare turned into a whopping $150 fare apiece! Mona's eyes bucked and bubbled. She wasn't sure if she'd now have enough to see the show they ran like a dizzy bat out of hell to see.

But she kept quiet about it. She didn't want to alarm Phyllis who was nervous about going in the first place.

Chapter 4

They got to the city with a good hour to kill, though Mona worried about how she could afford the tickets. At first she started to ask Phyllis, promising to pay her back. After all, she popped out her credit card like it was nothing on the train. Surely Phyllis would have mercy on her and pick up the tab for the tickets. At least until they got back home when she could pay her back. Each ticket was $79 dollars.

"How about if we hang out in this bar while we wait," Mona suggested. She could use a drink while she sorted things out.

They both sat their very round spreads up on a barstool, side by side, and let their eyes roll over the shelves of decorative bottles trying to read the labels at a foot's distance using their 15/40–20/5 vision.

"What'll it be ladies," asked a bartender casually attending to busy work, prepping for a mad rush still several hours off. By the way these two squinted at the shelves he could tell they weren't regulars, and this being regulars of any bar.

"I think I'll have the one in the middle," Mona said after a few minutes of intense squinting, pointing to a bottle among at least seventy others, though smack dab in the middle of the shelf.

The bartender turned around, a pencil behind one ear, and dressed shadily bartender-ish in a real glitzy t-shirt, baseball cap, and dark designer shades looked in the direction of where Mona pointed.

"This one?" he asked, pointing to a bottle in the vicinity of the middle, waiting for her to say something like 'no, to the left, up, down,' or preferably its name.

"Yes, the blue bottle," and Mona scrunched her eyes together, moving her body to look around the bartender, hoping to give a better description, one that might help the man recognize where she was pointing. Normally she'd go for more of the generic drinks such as Rum and Coke, but then normally she didn't drink. Only when her and Frank were out at a show might she order the Rum and Coke.

Mona turned to Phyllis, also crunching up her face waiting to be asked which one she wanted. "Isn't that a pretty color? I don't think I've ever seen a bottle that blue," she said.

"Well, I think that one on the other end is prettier." Phyllis turned to Mona, "it kind of looks like a sky blue doesn't it."

Mona's eyes slid across the rows of bottles finding the sky-blue bottle Phyllis was talking about. "Oh yeah, that one is pretty. Wonder what's in it…"

The bartender though, didn't make a move. This was a first. Two women, assuredly housewives, were acting like they were out shoe shopping, talking about bottle colors looking pretty and whatnot.

"Look ladies, as you can see, there are many bottles on the shelf. Maybe it might help if you told me what you want in your drink?" Paraphrasing the question had to be the solution here.

Mona spoke up, squirming on the stool a little too. "Well, what goes in the sky-blue one?"

Again the bartender turned around to find which bottle she was talking about. That figured, he mumbled to himself when he saw the Bombay Sapphire sitting on the end of the shelf. He was going to have to do what he did with countless of others who wandered in off the street having no idea what these colorful bottles they pointed out did to first timers who tried to drink them. Knocked them all flat on their butts was what happened.

He grabbed the Bombay off the shelf and tapped each glass with a drop of alcohol, just enough to give the white fruit juice he poured in the glasses in healthy proportions, a little Vodka flavoring.

"Would you like this with a twist of lemon or a cherry?" he asked robustly moving his arms as if he was concocting the all and out drink, when he was only wiping down the counter.

"How about both," Mona chirped, wiggling her butt more on the stool. She was just starting to feel fuzzy about being out. And to think, the drink hadn't even been poured yet.

The bartender dropped both a lemon and cherry in each glass and sat the drinks before them. "That'll be $15.00…" and without giving Mona a chance to wipe the fluid that almost sprayed out of her mouth away, he threw in, "…or do you want to open a tab?"

"Fifteen-dollars..." Mona gasped.

"Oh Mo—here…let me pay for this. You've been paying for everything," Phyllis offered, opening her large white Coach purse Joe had bought her to show up Frank for one of her birthdays.

"Oh my gosh," Mona muttered looking around and down at the floor, feeling as if she might pass out. She snapped up as Phyllis laid two twenties on the counter. "This had better be good," she scolded the smirking bartender, shaking her finger at him too.

Chapter 5

"Oh good heavens," sighed Phyllis, looking at a crowd that extended two city blocks. Looked like fans anxious to see a Beyoncé or Denzel performing. The mob was so large they couldn't see where the line ended, though they clearly saw where it began…right up front at the ticket window.

"Come on Phyl, follow me," Mona whispered. "We are getting in this show!"

"Oh no, you're not," growled a nearby woman, with her hair pulled up in a banana float. "Not busting in line ahead of me you're not!"

How Mona missed all that yellow hair standing so close by would remain a great banana float mystery yet to be told. She grabbed Phyllis by the arm, bouncing up and down, pretending she hadn't heard the woman, looking over heads as if she was trying to find the party they'd gotten separated from.

"Oh, there he is!" Mona shouted. "Look! He's way up there," and she pulled Phyllis along, who was holding her head, and hand, while muttering… '*who? There who is?*'

The crowd was smart though. Those along the path Mona plowed through kept a steady eye trained on them, waiting for them to reach 'there he is.'

"Tim, didn't you hear us calling you," Mona said yanking on the sleeve of a young guy with his hands in his pockets. She could feel the crowd's glare burrowed in her back.

Double Dare

The guy looked down at Mona, frowned, thought a minute, and then smiled. "Mom! I thought I told you to grab my jacket! My wallet was in my jacket pocket!"

Mona knew just what that meant. She was going to have to pay for Tim, and his date standing on the other side of him with her arm wrapped through his, peering over to see whom he was talking to.

"Awl Tim, you're so lame!" Someone behind them jeered.

"Yeah Tim! You don't know them, you punk!"

And, "Hey Mom! Here's your son over here…"

By the time they reached the ticket window the crowd managed to entertain themselves in a variation of mother and son skits. Tim and his date loved it. They played along, jeering back at the crowd. "Leave mom alone," and "mom don't love you anymore."

Mona wasn't laughing, at least not when she was hit with a whopping $379 bill to purchase all four tickets. She scrounged in her purse, one of her older more worn purses she slung around on weekends, looking for her emergency credit card. There was no way she could embarrass herself handing over a credit card that might not have the available funds on it.

The ticket agent took the card, swiped it, and Mona waited on pins and needles for the register tape to start tittering, making the sounds that the transaction had gone through. This was a card she hadn't touched. It was the card where she plunked a large amount of her earnings on, and occasionally fondled it when she changed purses, swearing one day when she finally got desperate enough to be daring, she'd use it.

Transaction approved, Tim and his date zipped by them and disappeared inside the theatre, while Phyllis wrapped her arms around her best friend and gave her the biggest kiss on the cheek.

"Thank you so much Mo—you don't know what this means to me!"

Mona appreciated the show of gratitude but the truth was, this quick trip to the show was costing her much more than a show and train ticket. Two-to-three hundred dollars she expected to spend. A thousand dollars slipped down the drain she hadn't. This wasn't exactly the daring fun she anticipated. Nothing yet felt good and fun. In fact, she felt sick to her stomach.

She looked over at Phyllis, her eyes caught in the flicker and flashes of animation dancing along with the music on stage. Phyllis was in her world trying to sing along, clapping her hands, and once springing out of the chair when Harvey came on, just as happy as a lark. Mona only wished she could have shared in Phyllis's enchantment because the show seemed like a lot of fun. Phyllis wasn't the only one shrieking out the tears of joy. The audience loved Hairspray.

But Mona already had her thoughts grinding into how she would replace the money. Three and a half possibles she had lined up. This was the almost daring excitement about her work. The possibles. She scoured business ventures looking for great ideas where she'd ping the venturist, promising she could triple their earnings. That's the only way she got paid, which right there was the dare, and adventure. Who would find pleasure in working their buns off for free?

That's what she sat there thinking about, as Phyllis and a theatre packed to sold-out capacity clapped and cheered, singing and shuffling their feet to the silliness being had on stage.

"What's wrong Mo—? This show is great…" and she gave her that supportive arm nudge, turning right back to the live animation.

That's when it hit Mona. She was the one trying to convince Phyllis to break out of the 'scared to live' cycle, and here she was sitting there thinking about work and possibilities of how she'd replace the money she just spent. Who really was the one scared to live, sitting there with a whopping $279,000 on a crisis card she planned to one day use when she gathered the courage to have fun.

Mona catapulted out of her seat, arms and hands flying up in the air, paradoxically causing a commotion as it wasn't the best timed. The audience moaned, and she even caught one of the performers looking over at her from a distant frown.

"Mo!" Phyllis hissed, snatching Mona back down in her seat. "What are you doing!?!"

"This is great," Mona gleamed, oblivious to a heavy girl crying. "Gosh…I love these performers."

They left the theatre laughing, bumping into each other and sharing highlights of the show; highlights Mona missed most of, and Phyllis saw all of.

"You know what," Mona broke through Phyllis's feverish rant about how great she thought Harvey was. "I'm going in that nail shop and having my nails done."

Phyllis piped down. She had her thrill, laughed her head off, and now she was ready to return home. She looked at her watch. "Well, what time does the train come?"

"I don't know...I think they run every few hours," Mona said checking her watch too. "But it shouldn't take long. A nail salon in the center of the city has to know what they're doing."

"But it's almost five," Phyllis cautioned. "I'd rather not travel in the dark."

Mona laughed and nudged Phyllis with that same supportive arm bump. "Are we scared of the boogey man?" she teased.

Phyllis, back to her pensive self, quietly walked across the street beside Mona, fearing the worst, but hoping for the best. Nail appointments typically didn't take longer than an hour, if that long. Plus, Mona might be right. These looked like real pros, at least by how elaborate the salon looked from the outside.

...and as it turned out, from the inside too. "Can you afford this," Phyllis asked, standing on Mona's heels speaking directly into the spine of her neck. "This place looks—"

"—Hello," came a dainty gaudy voice from behind a partially masculine shell. "How may we help you two today?"

Phyllis's eyes sat on Mona's shoulder watching a young man dressed in black from neck to toe listen to Mona explain how she and her friend were looking to have their nails done.

'We?' Phyllis thought. She didn't want a manicure. All she wanted was to get home before dark.

"Agh, I'm sorry, but our clinical specialists charge anywhere from $500 on up," the young partial man smugly informed Mona.

"A nail," Mona asked complimenting his smugness.

The young artisan rolled his eyes above his head. "No, to sit with," he tersely spat.

"To sit with and do what," Mona argued, wanting to snatch the little smug child out of the black leotards. Here activists of many creeds fought to prevent the very subtleties he saw fit to snub them with. If she looked him up in a glossary, he likely would be described as, happily excused hypocrite.

"I'm sorry, but you'll need an appointment to sit with one of our artists," he said, promptly zipping his mouth shut after his last word.

"No, you said I need $500 a damn nail!," Mona said raising her voice. "…And I have $500 a nail!"

Exasperation showing on his face he rolled his average eyes above his little pea head again. "Look, all of our artists require a $500 up front sitting fee, and an appointment!"

"Well I think you're lying to me because first you said I only needed $500 a nail, and now I need an appointment to sit with a clinical doctor that's now just an art person."

The confused young man, in more ways than one, started to walk away when what looked like a higher-ranking clinical artist approached the desk.

"Is there a problem here Jamie," asked a woman a lot stiffer than Jamie, wearing a black turtleneck and speaking without moving her lips.

"Yes there is a problem," Mona answered for Jamie. "First I'm told I only need $500 a nail to have my nails done. Next thing I hear is this business about needing an appointment to sit with a clinical doctor that come to find out is really just an art person."

The woman started to speak, drawing up this deep breath loaded full of policy malarkey. So Mona cut the woman off at the underpass again.

"Now, just so you know. I have $500 a damn nail. That is no problem. But I don't appreciate being lied to as I'm sure Jamie over here must know what it feels like being discriminated against!"

Fifteen minutes later Mona and Phyllis were being ushered into a private room separated by an oriental partition to undress behind.

Double Dare

"What did you do Mo? Rob a bank? How can you afford this," Phyllis asked hustling out of her pants and slipping into a heavy black robe lying on one of the two massage tables.

"I'm spending what is known as my emergency fun stash," Mona laughed. "So cha-ching! Cha-ching! I'm just scratching the surface here my friend. We have a long waaayyyss to go!"

Phyllis edged from around the partition. This did not sound good. Mona sounded like she'd been talking with a doctor ringing a lot of bells in her ear. No sane person would bust his or her nest egg open otherwise. Well, not unless they recently robbed a bank.

"I'm serious here Mo—where is this money coming from?"

"I'm serious too Phyl," Mona deviously smiled. "I decided to break open my piggy bank and spend some of my 'stay-at-home' marketing money."

"Oh Mo—no." And Phyllis started to untie the robe. "Let's get out of here. I'm not letting you spend the last of your only money."

There was a loud knock at the door and a heavy voice asking if they were ready. Quickly Phyllis retied the robe as a tall very handsome velvety man entered.

"Ladies, are you ready," this too good-looking-to-be-true person smiled.

"Right behind you, you dark and lovely child!"

Chapter 6

Nails manicured, body waxed, bathed, sunflower seed oiled and massaged they bounced gaily out of the Parle Duloup, hair waffling in the early evening wind more alive and animated than after leaving the theatre.

"Oh my goodness," Phyllis sang, throwing her arms out and twirling around, "I feel so light on my feet." She turned to Mona, who was smiling and feeling light in the head herself, and asked, "Do you feel lighter?" And without waiting on her answer she went on, "it feels like if a real good breeze were to come by right now, I'd blow away!"

Mona beamed. She felt the same way too. She had mocked those artists calling themselves technicians and clinical doctors and specialists and so forth, when they really were. They gave them the works, and really didn't charge as much as she expected, though by this point in the living venture, she hardly cared about cost. If Phyllis only knew, she was just getting started. The night had yet to begin. The surface of her crisis stash hadn't even yet flinched.

"Ooo, let's go in here," Mona said, seeing a runway of handbags in a Paris Deluxe window. "I wanna get me a new bag. I feel like an old lady carry this big 'ole raggedy thing."

They went inside, leaving the dark skies behind, trading it for brilliant lights and top of the line designer fashion handbags.

"Hello ladies," greeted an older and less attractive, though friendlier version of Jamie. "How are we doing this evening?"

"Don't worry," Phyllis quickly chuckled, "she can afford it," she cackled. "She can buy one of every one of these bags off your hands if you let her."

The associate's eye lit up, and he smiled. "Well, then let me show you ladies around," and immediately he sashayed behind the counter.

"I want the one behind you," Mona said without giving him a chance to lift up from beneath the counter with his latest bags. Mona turned to Phyllis, "Isn't that one sharp?"

"Which one?" It was hard to separate the not so sharp bags from the sharp ones. All of them looked the same—gorgeous.

The associate lifted up with three bags swinging on his arm, to look up to where Mona pointed. "Ah yeah, the Burberry. That one is a favorite around here." He used a pole with a hook on the end to bring it down. "Every girl has one of these. You won't pass a night where you won't see at least one woman carrying one just like it."

"Mo—you don't want to be carrying a purse that everyone is carrying, do you?"

"But I like it," and she ran her hand over its smooth leather, opening it to look inside. "Looks heavy, but it feels like carrying butter."

The associate and Phyllis watched her eyes maul the bag, giving her time to flirt with a grand's worth of danger before the associate started laying on the counter his real arsenal. It looked like he was just moving in the shop and unpacking when he finished toppling the counter with bags so fine and pricey Phyllis had to bring Mona to her senses.

"Mo—! Now where in the hell will you carry that bag? You barely leave the house as it is."

The associate knew he had the ladies at this point. These were his favorite customers. Women who went nowhere, but whom always dreamed of going big places. "You'll love this one," he coyly said, slipping one of his newcomer ostrich bags on the counter.

Mona's eyes fell like falling feathers over the bag. "Oh my God," she sighed as if she just entered heaven. "You are my savior. It's perfect."

Five minutes and forty-eight hundred dollars later Mona was dumping the contents from her old bag on the counter, and telling the associate to get rid of the old bag. Dressed in the snazzy ripped t-shirt and jeans, the doll of an ostrich handbag went with everything.

"What time is it," Phyllis asked, not bothering to check her wrist. Something about this magical moment felt so right. Like what they were doing was perfectly normal. An experience owed to every person at least once during his or her journey.

"I don't know but I'm starved!" Mona said as if they deserved more. "What do you say we get something to eat before hopping on the train?"

That time Phyllis looked down at her wrist, but only to see if it would be worth their while to find a decent restaurant. She didn't like going to restaurants after 9pm.

"It's a quarter of. I wonder what time restaurants close around here?"

"Oh, this is the city that never sleeps. We'll find—ooo! Look! Let's go over there. I'm feeling up for some good Italian food."

"Good choice," Phyllis said. She found it easy to pick a dish off an Italian menu. Plus, dark restaurants always made a moment seem more magical.

The hostess at the door didn't seem to share their enthusiasm however. New hairdos, French manicures, and that forty-eight hundred dollar bag swung over Mona's shoulder aside, Ms. Twiggy looked them up and down as if they might be carrying a strange disease.

"We'll take a table for two," Mona said.

"Do you have reservations," the snob snapped.

"Look at us," Mona said. "Do we look like we need reservations," and she swung her purse around for Ms. Twiggy to get a good looksee, as she cheekily laughed with Phyllis. "And they said we have attitude!"

Ms. Twiggy looked at the bag, actually her eyes got hooked on the bag, but she played it off, trying to act like that Ostrich swung over her shoulder was no big deal. She rolled her eyes and walked away, to end up at the bar area, really leaning into the bartenders trying to get her face back. She made sure Mona and Phyllis knew exactly what she was laughing at, and who, that night, would not be getting seated.

"I don't know Mo—but I don't care to eat in places where I'm not welcomed."

"Me neither," Mona said while keeping her eye on Ms. Twiggy. "I don't need reality TV to tell me exactly what goes on in these type of places. I didn't agree with sit-ins back in the day either, and for damn sure am not settling for it today!"

The hostess switched back over to them, to spill an apology on their newly manicured feet, following her glib regrets by offering them a seat at the bar.

"Isn't that where all the creeps sit," Phyllis asked, looking at a dark area where one brooding patron sat.

"Ugh...you're right Phyl—it does look like an area where only creeps sit," Mona said, returning to address the impatiently waiting hostess.

"That's okay. My friend is right. This place looks a little creepy. We thought this was an upscale place, not Mel's Diner!" Mona spun around and accidentally bumped into Phyllis grinning and trying to get a good look at the sideshow being entertained by Neil Diamond and all of China's fine China.

"How about that?" Mona laughed as they headed down the street, looking for a friendlier atmosphere. "You might want to thank me. I think I just saved us a couple hundred bucks and a stomach flu!"

They settled on a little Tribeca Indian restaurant splicing the air with Hindu metallic sounds pixelating the ambiance. It was the kind of reverberations not meant to hang beneath for any length of time. Too long beneath this canopy of music and they could end up seeing colorful squares and circles for the rest of their natural life.

It was almost 9:30 when Phyllis next looked at her watch. "I think I better call Joe and let him know where I am." She didn't look worried as much as she looked ready to have responsible fun.

Mona looked at her watch too. "Oh, it's not even half-time yet. Don't interrupt him."

"Yeah, I guess you're right. What time do the games normally end anyway?" She had been having so much fun she forgot the timing ritual she used to time when Joe would fall in the house.

"Midnight," Mona answered doing some thinking of her own.

"I probably should order a take-out platter for Joe, in case he's hungry when he gets in," Phyllis said, using up the silent space where Mona was orchestrating the next phase of their fun.

"Frank hates this food," Mona idly replied, tapping her cell phone in rapid irrevocable strokes.

"Do you think we'll get home before midnight?" Phyllis was now beginning to worry.

Mona looked up wearing the scariest smile Phyllis had yet seen. "Oh no," Phyllis said, defensively holding up both hands before Mona could speak. "No more…that's it. We're going home after this!"

"Yes, we sure are," Mona gleamed wildly, "in this!" and she shoved the phone in Phyllis's face.

Phyllis rumbled around in her purse looking for her glasses to see what was on the small screen. Just to be sure she cleaned her lens, to make sure she was seeing what she thought she saw. That couldn't be a car… a shiny G37 convertible Infiniti type car!?!

"I've always wanted one," Mona said like she'd lost the one remaining logical cell in her head.

"Mo—it's freakin' 9:30 at night! Where are you going to find a car at this hour!?!"

"Check!" Mona shouted over top of Phyllis's head as she took the phone from the disoriented Phyllis.

Quickly she tapped the screen, in more of those rapid irrevocable strokes, bringing the phone up to her ear waiting for the other end to pick up.

"Ugh yes, hello, this is Mona. I found your ad on the Internet and want to drop by this evening to take that Infiniti off your hands…huh? …Well yes I'm buying it. I'm out here in the city now and need something like this to get home."

Mona covered the mouthpiece to whisper to one stunned Phyllis. "Don't worry. This thing will have us home in no time. It's a six—" and she moved her hand

Double Dare

away from the phone. "Oh, sure. That's no problem," she smiled with a straight face. "Can you repeat your address again…ugh…okay, so that's 36999 Lovers Lane? Man, that should be easy to find."

Phyllis threw up her hands. Mona was gone. They should've never eaten at the Tribeca because between the spicy food and twanging music, one or the other had filled her dear friend's head with those circles and squares.

"So what did he say?" Phyllis asked as Mona ended the call, hoping to God it was one word—No!

"She…" Mona clarified, "…said to come on over. These are the directions," she said, showing Phyllis the piece paper she jotted the address down on. A straight line with an arrow pointed to the one word: Car!

"You're—" Phyllis couldn't even get out the words. Mona had to be kidding. "Mo, please tell me you aren't seeing circles and squares!?!" And she raised her hand. "Never mind, I don't know why I would ask a crazy person if they've lost their mind."

But Mona hadn't lost her mind. She grabbed the waiter she'd been flirting with throughout their meal; a thin, dark-skin Indian man. "Listen Poo…tell your boss I'll add a hundred bucks to your tip, plus pay for your gas if you take me to this address." She pointed to the screen on her phone.

Poorvaj looked down at the screen and back over to her, and then to Phyllis as if he was verifying if he needed to be concerned. When he got no unmistakable warning signs, he rushed off to share Mona's offer with his boss.

Phyllis clapped her hands, as if the sound would jar Mona to her senses. "Mo! Please get a hold of yourself!"

But Mona had gotten a hold of herself, and some fun along the way. She was not to be dissuaded. She flew behind Poorvaj slipping out of his apron, calling over her shoulder, "come on Phyl! I'm not crazy. I'm going to teach the both of us a little about living!"

"You wreck it, you buy it," the owner told Poorvaj as he handed him the keys. Those women were acting mighty strange to him. No telling where, and how, poor Poorvaj's jolly night might end.

Poorvaj lead Mona and Phyllis through a back exit into a very muggy smelly alley. In the dark murky grim and grime sat a beautiful cranberry Mercedes; a late model sedan. All three climbed inside and drove to the address Mona found in the Internet search for the car of her dreams. 36999 Lovers Lane.

Chapter 7

Anyone else and the bank would've shut down their account and declined all their purchases beyond the train tickets. But not for Mona. For some reason the bank wasn't catching these wild transactions coming in at one, two, three, and four thousand dollar clips. Now there's the car, and Mona's telling a wealthy debutant and her father looking over her shoulder, she would put the entire cost of the car on her credit card…the credit card intravenously dwindling her fun should she happen to live to the ripe old age where she reasoned she'd be too old to enjoy.

The wealthy debutant and her father didn't bat an eye. They called their banker family member over and sitting right there in their lovely beast of a living room completed the transaction. A $70,000 wallop they knocked out of Mona's account, and she didn't bat an eye. She sat there smiling and nodding and humming at every word that left their mouth. At this point, there was no doubt she did not expect to live long. At least not long enough to ever experience this much spur of the moment fun.

They left the mansion about 10:30pm with papers and keys to a luxury silver convertible in hand. It was a beauty, even Phyllis acknowledged this part.

"That is a car to die for," Phyllis said, having cashed in some of her reasoning too. What the heck! Mona's upbeat attitude was infectious. "Now if only I could go out and buy a car this quickly," she said sliding in the fresh white cotton perfumed car.

The young debutant and her father leaned over to give Mona their parting good-byes. "You know where we live. Please, if anything at all goes wrong, just give us a call, or stop by...okay?"

They both stood up and took a small step away from the car, as if synchronized dancers. Waving the Green Acres signature greeting, they also smiled.

Mona sat still for a while; Phyllis thinking she was taking in the moment. As it was, it was a lot to take in. The car was absolutely stunning; the buttery leather seats, rich paneling, and the latest dashboard trinkets. Enough to make a dreamer believe they were inside the cabin of an actual Dreamliner.

But no matter how spectacular the Dreamliner, sitting in the car ten minutes with those Green Acres people waving like frozen kaleidoscopic manikins, was just too long.

"What's wrong," Phyllis asked. She sort of hoped this was the part when Mona had her 'ah ha' moment and the both of them returned to their senses.

"I don't know how to drive a stick shift," Mona said, quickly turning to Phyllis to ask, "Do you?"

'Oh dear Lord, and Heavens forbid!' Phyllis hadn't driven a stick shift either. Phyllis didn't even drive. She only used her driver's license once, to show to an ABC store clerk. But to some avail, in a way it was a happy moment. Mona could now return the keys, tear up the contract, and they catch the train back home.

"Oh my gosh Phyl, I'm so embarrassed. Why don't you roll down your window and tell those people they can go back inside."

"Huh?"

"Never mind." Mona fumbled with the gadgets around her to roll down the window. Accidentally she ended rolling down all four, but that was okay. At least she had the main window rolled down.

She gaily waved the Green Acres pair back over to the car. "Ugh…I'm trying to call my husband…so I might be a minute here…" she said, wanting to add, 'so you can go inside now.' "…Thanks again," she said, in effect telling them they could now go inside.

"Oh, okay," the daughter chirped. "Be safe!"

Mona pressed some of the gadgets that rolled all the windows down, to end up rolling up two windows and turning on the windshield wipers. The horn went off too, which she quickly fixed by turning the car off. The only problem now, two windows remained down; the back window, and her window. Plus the wipers were still going.

She gaily waved again at the Green Acres pair who turned around. "…be safe…" Mona muttered, turning to Phyllis to announce why she was so displeased by that inane send-off greeting.

"When have you seen a greeting card like that!?!"

"What?" Phyllis was still trying to figure out when she'd find the right gadget to stop the wipers. It looked kind of silly sitting out in this handsome dry night with wipers going storm crazy.

"Why do people insist on barfing those silly asinine regurgitations!?! Does she think we plan to pull out of here and drive into the hands of carjackers!?!"

Now that really was funny. Phyllis shook her head. She hadn't thought about it that way. "I think this one is for the wipers," Phyllis said leaning over to stop the wipers while Mona ranted on.

"How's this one?" and Mona changed her voice for mimicking purposes. "Be safe…don't get hurt if your plane crashes! Be safe…try to outrun a tornado if you see, or hear about one coming. If you run…take your guns with you for safe travel…but be safe! Like really? Why do people insist on saying stupid shit!?!'

"Mo—I think it's a harmless goodwill wish," Phyllis said, actually seeing exactly how it applied to Mona in the given circumstance, and WHY she should heed it. She was going to need it when she faced Frank.

"Well just as soon as I get home I'm going to send a greeting card of my own. It's going to say, be safe, don't slip and break your leg!"

"Mo—how are you going to get us home?"

Mona looked up. The smiling robotic Green Acres people had gone inside. "I actually read about how you're supposed to drive clutches." She turned the car on and put it in reverse to back it out of the driveway. Everything went smooth sailing there. The first gearshift glided smoothly into one slot…no hiccups there… but then she put her foot on the gas to go.

Chapter 8

It was after 11:00pm and they made it as far as the next mansion over from where they started. Phyllis's heart sat in her throat the entire time the car lurched and jerked all of a hundred or so yards. There was no way they were getting anywhere near the ninety-six more miles they needed to drive.

"You know what? I'm calling for a tow. Maybe we can get towed to a rest stop," Mona said clearly seeing there was no way they were getting any further than where they were.

"And then what?"

"Well," and she sighed heavily. "I guess then I'll just have to call Frank."

And that's just what they did, tacking an additional $500 onto Mona's skyrocketing tab.

"Joe is going to kill me when he gets here," Phyllis said, sort of staring into parts of her after-life. "I know him...he is going to really ream me for this one."

"Awl...just tell him I made you do it...which when you think about it, I did. So blame me," Mona shrugged, after enduring Frank for twenty minutes asking what in the hell she'd done.

He was so enraged he didn't even realize it wasn't his money she was spending. Well, technically it was his money, but legally it wasn't. He did explode when she explained the car part, but he only roared on about how she got stranded in a city of six million people, at the stroke of midnight, driving a new luxury car she couldn't even drive! That was the crazy baffling part. It wasn't as if she was around the corner with her keys stuck in the ignition of her old Toyota Corolla, with the doors locked, like she'd done several times. No! She was stranded in a city of six million people, at the stroke of midnight, over 96-miles away!

"But really Phyl—didn't some of today feel good?"

Phyllis thought for a second. Yes, some of the day did feel good. But, if only they could've stopped after dinner. That's where Mona went too far. She certainly didn't feel so good sitting in a highly trafficked rest stop leaning over as far as she could to talk, because she thought a creep might be lurking nearby.

"I think I just need to go home and sleep this one off," was the way Phyllis put it.

"Oh Phyl, please not you too. Don't do this to me. Not after what I've done to make this day special for you. I've got to have someone on my side when Frank gets here."

And yeah, she was going to need someone on her side when Joe got there too. Phyllis reached across the table taking Mona's hands in hers. They were ice cold, but hers were warm. She shook her hands to pass on how much she really appreciated what she tried to do.

"Mona, what you've given me today will last a lifetime. Trust me on that. So thanks friend. I really do owe you one," and she laughed, "As soon I get ready to start throwing in that towel, you're going to be the first person I call to take along for that ride!"

Mona pulled her hands away and laughed. She knew she'd gone overboard. But she just couldn't stop herself. Something got a hold of her and told her to go, go, go. In a way she wished she hadn't obeyed that instinct, but something else she couldn't put a finger on kept driving her forward. Made it all seem so right.

A middle-aged woman walking slowly behind an elderly woman pushing a walker started to pass by. They stopped near Mona and Phyllis, looking around for a place to sit. At midnight all of the tables were full, as if it was a holiday, when rest stops were known for being notoriously busy.

Mona tapped the woman on the forearm. "Miss, why don't you both sit here?"

But the woman looked down and hesitated before speaking. "Are you sure it's okay?" She was desperate, but decent. She wasn't content on taking handouts.

"Of course. We'll sit out in the lobby." It was a little clammier out in the lobby area with it being so close to the latrines, but clean enough to wait for however long it might take Frank and Joe to get there and rescue them.

"Why can't we all sit here," argued a scraggily voice pushing the walker.

"Mother," the woman leaned over to scold the scraggily voice that probably always spoke up. "They don't want to share their conversation with us." And she smiled at Mona and Phyllis as if asking that they excuse her mother for speaking out.

"Yeah, why not," Phyllis said scooting over. "Come on and scoot in here with us and share some of this once-in-a-lifetime fun," she joked.

The woman looked alarmed, as if she had a second reason to decline the offer. But not her mother. She took not a step further, knocking the walker into the table and sliding down on the bench beside Phyllis.

"Celia, see if they're selling some gin around here," the mother quipped, hands quivering as she fumbled in her pockets to pull out a tissue. "I need a drink to wash down these pills."

The daughter had no choice but to join them, even if she didn't follow her mother's request to find her a drink. Uneasily she sat beside Mona, with half a cheek on the bench, deciding not to say much.

"Do you know what these pills do to you," asked the mother unraveling a pill from the napkin. "They make you think you were a baby all over again," she laughed without waiting for a reply.

"Mother!" gasped the daughter.

"Oh hush! These girls are out having fun. Didn't you hear nothing they said? People out having fun don't care about no old woman wetting herself."

"You know that's how the life cycle goes," said the woman bobbing her head around to look at Phyllis as she dropped the pill in her mouth.

"That's how life naturally goes. You come out the womb babbling in diapers, needin' to be looked after, and you go back in the ground the same way. That's why you girls are right to be out here having fun."

"Too bad everyone hasn't caught on to living," the mother went on to say, lifting an eye to put on her daughter. "I try to tell them all the time but they just don't listen until it's too late."

There wasn't much to say to that so Mona and Phyllis kept quiet, though trading looks. The daughter didn't look so happy, but the mother talked, and looked as if she'd lived a full good life.

"I sent it all," Mrs. Corinthia went on, needing no encouragement to explain how she made it through war times cheering up soldiers. She and other single girls, some married women too, sang to the guys, read letters from loved ones to them, and partied all night long with those able-bodied enough to party.

"I had my fun and lived my life…and try to tell all my children to do the same…" the mother said.

But by the tightness of the daughter's face it didn't look as if she'd taken her mother's advice. There was little doubt if Mona and Phyllis weren't there she would have reminded her mother not to forget those paying the costs to foot her happy bill of life.

"Please, I'm sorry. If we're bugging you I can find us another table," the daughter spoke up, deliberately interrupting her mother's wartime stories.

Double Dare

"No...your mother is fine. I love hearing feel good stories," Phyllis said, resting her chin in the palm of her hand, charmed by the mother.

"Yes," Mona chimed in, "I think a messenger sent your mother to speak her words of wisdom to us."

This still didn't seem to convince the daughter who worked all day before committing to drive 349-miles round-trip to remove her mother from a senior daycare she felt was not up to par.

"So, you wanna know what's it like?" the mother said waggling her head to look over at Phyllis.

"Huh? Ugh, I mean excuse me ma'am...but what's what like?"

"You want to know what dying is like," the mother flatly asked.

"Mother!"

"What? What's so wrong about asking that?" Mona asked, trying to calm the daughter.

But to no avail. The daughter quickly reminded her mother about her long day, and how much further she had to drive the 'tail end' of her life to the new place where she'd be staying.

"Gosh Mo—I'm not too sure I want to know what that feels like," Phyllis sighed, sadly shaking her head.

"That's why we have to live now...so it doesn't feel so bad," Mona said, a little glad too, that the daughter scooped her mother when she did. Who wanted to be sad when they hadn't yet fully lived?

"Come on, let's get out of here, and sit somewhere else. These people in here are depressing me," Mona said hopping up.

"No Mo! This is it! I'm not going anywhere else! Joe and Frank are—"

"—Goodness Phyl! I just meant let's sit out in the lobby! But that's just what that angel was sent over here to help you see," Mona fussed. "You're so afraid of dying, that you're too afraid to live."

"Oh now, that's so unfair," Phyllis moped, following Mona out into the lobby. "I just don't want to die trying to live!"

Mona plopped down on the sole vacant bench in the lobby, throwing her feet up. "So tell me…what one thing we did today that came close to dying?"

Phyllis plopped down on the opposite end of the bench and threw her feet up too. It tickled her when she thought about it though.

"Well…" she giggled, "we almost died running for that train?"

"Oh no, that one doesn't count," Mona said. "The healthiest person in the world can drop dead of a heart-attack!"

"I just don't want to live my life with any regrets," Phyllis sighed, still creeped-out by the daughter and mother visit.

"That's funny," Mona reflected back too. "Did you happen to notice who seemed to be living with all the regrets?"

"I know…" Phyllis sighed, unable to get the images out of her head. The mother sounded so upbeat, up against the deadbeat daughter. "For 98- years old you have to give it to her. She looked great!"

"But that's just it," Mona thoughtfully sat up to add, "that's exactly how you are Phyl!" Yes, it was exactly how Phyllis was, a worrywart just like the daughter.

"Unt un…no," Phyllis said sitting upright too. "I am not like that! No, I'm not!"

Mona laughed. "You mean you don't want to be like that, because you are exactly like that. Wait until we get home. As a matter of fact, as soon as you see Joe, you're going to go right back to being careful about what you say and do," Mona laughed, continuing on to tease Phyllis, over-talking her weak defenses.

"Just keep looking at your fingers, and hands. They are going to start hardening and wrinkling up just like that daughter's hands."

"That is so not true," Phyllis muttered in a weak limp huff. She tried to think back. Was she really like that? And all be damn if when she got older she looked like that!

Mona looked at her watch. It was getting really late, 30-minutes later than she expected Frank to be there. Phyllis noticed the time too. But she was trying hard not to worry. It didn't stop her from shifting in the corner though, trying to find a way to keep her eyes on the creepy travelers moving around them, instead of thinking about sleep.

Mona was doing the same. She didn't want their fun to end that way either. That's how they came up with counting and laughing at travelers rushing into the lobby and dancing their way to the restrooms.

"Here comes another one..." Phyllis laughed, "can she make it...can she make it? She's a hopping...and she's a hoping..." and they broke out laughing watching the traveler dancing from foot to foot, entertaining them in a spin as she disappeared into the restroom.

"Don't you think they should have been here by now," Mona worried after a while, wringing her hands, wondering when one of the dancing travelers would turn into two spinning tops storming the lobby.

But by then Phyllis had made herself comfortable, reclined in a corner of the bench with her feet propped up over the top smiling about how Joe and Frank had probably spent 20-minutes discussing how angry they were, another 20-minutes speculating about the traffic they would run into, and now were probably at a gas station fussing about the cost of gas.

Chapter 9

Little did Mona and Phyllis know, their husbands had been held up, but for none of the reasons Phyllis waved away. The police pulled them over for speeding, just a few miles from the rest stop.

"Sir, were you in an accident earlier today," the leading police officer asked, a short square head man who didn't have far to bend to lean into the car.

"Accident?" Frank asked bewildered, immediately thinking they were about to become famous, entangled in another police scandal. "No sir. We've been at a sports bar all evening and just got a call from our wives about being towed and stranded at that rest stop."

All the square-head officer heard was the one most important word in the annuals of police literature. Bar. These men had been out drinking, and now they were driving…and speeding no less. They were treading the cusp of a possible conviction, and sure night in jail. The officer leaned further in the car, making the character Herman Munster come alive for Frank and Joe, trying to sniff the faintest smell of alcohol. One whiff and hog-tied and logged in it would be for these two.

"Sports bar huh," the officer asked, looking around the car for any other impeaching signs to pack onto his drinking and driving and speeding conviction.

Frank leaned away, but only because he couldn't take much more of looking Herman Munster so close in the face. "Yes, we watched the championship game tonight,"

Frank repeated, trying to stay calm while Joe sat quietly in the passenger seat, trying to commit the dialogue to memory. Like Frank, he too expected he'd soon be repeating this story.

The officer lifted up from the window and returned to his cruiser with Frank's credentials; his driver's license, registration, and insurance card.

"Man, I'm a little nervous. I think they're gonna try and pull a Rodney King on us here tonight," Frank seethed over the sweat beads populating his forehead.

"Man no! Did you get a load of that bucket?" Joe chuckled, shaking his own head. "I don't wanna look, but what's the size of this other joker's head standing over here to my 3:15?"

There was another officer, much taller, who joined the search and seize party. He was standing on the right side of the car, just feet behind the passenger door, holding a flashlight to the back of Joe's head. The floodlight was in addition to the patrol car's high beams turned loose on the car, and the high-mast street lamps igniting the highway.

But Frank wasn't in a jovial mood. "I know thing, they might want to go ahead and haul me in now to save themselves an extra trip back out because I'm going to kill Mo when I see her," Frank angrily replied.

Joe couldn't help it. He burst out laughing, rocking in his seat and slapping his knee he got so tickled by the thought. He was thinking the same thing about Phyllis. What in the hell were those two thinking? Hope they had a good time because it wouldn't be anytime in Phyllis's near future she would hear that phrase coming out of her mouth again—good time.

The officer standing guard heard the commotion and moved closer to the car to look inside to see what the laughing was all about. Tapping the glass he asked Joe to roll the window down.

"You got jokes in there buddy," the leftover officer asked, leaning over the passenger door, brandishing two bushy brows and sawed off teeth.

Still laughing and wiping his eyes Joe went on and told the officer what Frank said. Both of them looked over at Frank, not amused, to enjoy harmonized laugh.

"Take it easy over there fella," the officer laughed, practically laying his head on Joe's shoulder. When he caught his breath, he lifted up and looked around to take another punch at Frank.

"What, you thought the priest was kidding about that for better or worse clause?"

Both men howled again, as the square-head officer sauntered back to the car. "Did you say both of your wives were towed to that rest stop just up ahead?"

"Yes, I did," Frank said through gritted teeth, now sure Mona wasn't pulling out of this one breathing all the way.

"Was it a silver car that was towed?" The officer asked, trying to hold his laughter.

Frank finally released his grip on the anger some and turned to face the grinning officer. "I have no idea what color the car is. But you might have a clear description of it shortly."

"My brother called me about it earlier," the officer matter-of-factly offered. "He said this woman bought a car brand new she couldn't even drive. He towed them all the way from Chesham Valley. Was that your wife," and the officer belted out a hearty laugh. "Oh buddy, I feel for you buddy…"

The officers felt so bad for Frank that they didn't issue him a citation. They just weren't that heartless. They even escorted him to the rest stop where the car was parked. Led Frank right up to the car while Mona and Phyllis were inside the lobby wondering what was taking them so long to get there.

"Awl man, this is nice," Joe said running his hand over the shiny finish, sparkling like a large diamond beneath what had to be the brightest lamppost on the parking lot. It was a real beauty. But damn! He didn't know they had it like that. Here he was buying Phyllis little 18-karat bracelets and whatnot, when they could afford to roll like this.

The officer turned off the patrol car's headlights and joined Joe, and somewhat Frank, to admire the brand new silver G37 toy Mona purchased.

"Yeah, the guys down at the station got a kick out of this call when it came in," laughed the sturdy-head officer, leaning over to peek inside the car. He was looking at the gearshift to see if it was as the call came in…an automatic gearshift.

Double Dare

"Yeah, we were sent out to check on it because it's not every day, in fact it's been no day someone bought a brand new car like this and couldn't drive it! Ha. Ha. Ha. And just like a woman she called 911 for a tow!"

"She called 911?" Frank asked incredulously.

"911 buddy."

Frank really didn't know what to think. The car was definitely beautiful. All he could think was maybe Mona hit the tables at the casino and left that part out. Maybe she was saving that part to surprise him with.

"Man, look at them rims. I know for a fact them rims costs a couple of grand, apiece, alone!" Joe stood back rubbing his chin and nodding, admiring the car at a distance. And "Chewwww..." he whistled, shaking his head too.

"I sure hope," and he stopped talking. These may have been two of the friendliest lawmen he ever met, but their immediate future still was up for grabs. There were only two types of people on earth he knew not to trust, and one of them was a police officer.

"I take it this is a surprise to you," the officer said smiling at Frank, relishing the look on his face. These were the high treasures of police work. Rarely did people like Frank and Joe materialize on an otherwise slow night.

Frank couldn't do anything but nod in agreement. There was no way Mona and Phyllis were in the rest stop. They had to be bound and gagged in the trunk. He was about to ask the officer to use his billy club to pop the trunk when the officer interrupted what he was sure was some damn good detective thinking.

"Say...we're about to turn in for the night. What do you say you teach your wives a little lesson?"

That was a good one too. Frank hadn't thought of that one. For Mona to pull this stunt, she deserved to be taught a lesson. He was all ears.

"Me and Officer Stayton over here will go in there and tell your wives the car was reported stolen... demand the keys...and bring them over to the station where you both can get even with them. Sound like a winner, buddy?"

"I like it," Joe cheered. He still wasn't through with Phyllis for going along with all of this.

"But, she did purchase it?" Frank asked, still trying to put the puzzle together.

"Oh yeah, that all checked out. The owners live not too far away. Up there in Chesham Valley. They said the women paid with a credit card."

A credit card, Frank thought. Was Mona hiding money from him? The most he remembered they had on their highest credit card was $7500, which was just about maxed out.

"Go ahead over to the station. It's straight up the highway at the next exit. You'll see it. The sign will say Highway Police Barracks," the officer informed them. "We'll go in and get them and bring them there in a few minutes."

Double Dare

Frank and Joe did as instructed. They hopped back in the car and peeled off the parking lot, headed to the police barracks. And the officers, Stayton and square-head Novell, did similar. They headed towards the lobby of the rest stop to greet the capriciously waiting, and diligently watching, Mona and Phyllis reclined on a brown bench.

Chapter 10

"Oh look," Mona sat up when she saw the officers walk into the lobby. "Maybe we should ask them if they heard anything about any motorists being stranded on the highway."

"You mean like after they make their little pit stop," Phyllis snickered, stilled lounged back on the bench having tucked her arms inside her blouse for warmth and comfort…with her eyes all the way closed.

"No, these two don't look like they're making any pit stops. Their stroll is much too leisure. Looks like they're looking for someone."

Quickly she turned to Phyllis who had her eyes, on her way to sleep heaven. "You know Phyl—we could've been sitting here all this time while someone was in here robbing the place blind, and didn't even know it!"

"Ha. Ha," Phyllis chuckled, nesting back with her feet kicked up as if it was high noon and they were out at the mall with a flat tire waiting on a ride home. "You mean like us," she blithely teased.

But Mona wasn't kidding. Her eyes grew rounder with each step the officers took, reaching the size of two caskets by the time they stopped in front of her. It was like something out of TV, just before receiving the worst news of her life.

"Excuse me ladies. Does that silver G37 convertible Infiniti belong to either of you?"

Double Dare

Slowly Mona rose. "Yes, it's my car," she said, heart thumping, already sure by the tone of the officer's voice something was very wrong. It may have not been Frank at all, but those rich Green Acres people instead. They could have reported the car stolen, or more like it, they probably stole the car themselves. How many times had she been warned about not buying off the Internet?

"—We're going to need you both to come down the station with us. That car was reported stolen," said the shorter officer, clearly the tougher one in the lead.

She knew it! Damn it! All those warnings and she had to be the foolish hardhead to go out and do just what she'd been warned not to do, and now look!

"What!?!" she near screamed, as Phyllis sat up to sing in a keynote just a pitch beneath her, "wha—"

"Oh no, siree Bob," Mona said in a steady voice. Truth was, she was about to go off. "I bought that car fair and square," she said going for the contract.

"Ma'am please! Take your hands out of the purse. You can show it to the captain down at the station. We have orders to bring you both in for questioning."

Mona looked back at Phyllis slowly standing up. "Can you believe this?" And she looked at the officers, tears welling up in her eyes. "Let me call my husband," she said, reaching again to open her purse.

"Ma'am! I don't want to have to arrest you for disobeying a lawful order, so please! If you want to save yourself from being embarrassed, you'll close that purse and come with us to sort all this out, down at the station!"

63

Slowly Mona and Phyllis followed the officers out of the lobby and onto the parking lot. Their problems were a lot larger than that one officer, Officer Novell's head. All Mona could think of was how she was going to explain this to Frank. Man! That officer's head didn't look so large after all.

Her knees wobbled and buckled as she followed the officers. Correct that. Both of their knees wobbled and buckled following the officers to the parking lot. Phyllis's knees got so wonky on her that she had to lean on Mona for support.

"Do you have the keys," the officer turned and asked Mona.

"Yes," Mona angrily replied. "But is it okay for me to reach in my purse and get them out or will this be enough to charge and arrest me on?"

When she got out of this one, she was going to give those Green Acres people a big piece of her mind. And she was going to do something about the Internet too. That's where these police officers needed to be. Surfing the lawless high-fi wires victimizing innocent citizens like her and Phyllis.

"Mo, please don't say any more," Phyllis quivered, so faint from worry she thought she was seeing in triples. She saw her entire 6395-square-footage of a house in that man's one head. Never in her life had she been involved in breaking one infraction with the law. Not even for so much as one traffic ticket.

Double Dare

Officer Stayton took the keys and slid in the car behind the wheel. He looked too big to be in her car. Almost as if it was his car! One foot outside the car, and the other inside, she watched him turn the ignition with one large hand. With the other matching hand he toggled the gearshift she had struggled with.

"This way ladies," she heard behind her, turning around to find Officer Novell had the back door to his cruiser sprung wide open, and him gesturing with a clubby hand for them to get in.

Mona and Phyllis had no choice. They had to do what they would be doing for the very first time in their newest career of fun, and climb inside the back of a police car. Phyllis cried a bucket of tears after she settled in the seat. This was a nightmare growing to sizeable proportions. She was about to join a glee club singing a surreal new version of fun.

A few minutes later they found themselves rolling to a stop at a building that didn't exactly resemble the police barracks they had in mind. They were thinking bricks and something in the beige-tannish coloring scheme. Not a tin metal building with little silver letters spelling Highway Patrol Visitor's Center.

Officer Novell turned to look in the back seat at the both of them staring in opposite directions. "By chance, did you say your husbands were on their way to pick you up?"

Mona heard his voice first. "Yes I did," she quickly responded. Finally! Finally he heard something she said.

Something that had been weighing heavy on her mind. And still, regardless, she was suing them all. The Green Acres people for stealing and then selling them a stolen car. The train station for not following their own rules and putting them off the train when they found out they didn't have the proper fare. The sly bartender. He probably spiked their drinks. That's why they were acting irrational like this. These highway patrol people were getting sued too. Since when did plain average everyday women commit these types of crimes? They knew they weren't thieves. They didn't even know how to run. Any ordinary person could look at them and tell they were ordinary wives who loved their husbands and tastefully decorated their homes.

And for darn sure the Internet was getting sued. Oh boy. The Wide-world of Interneting was getting sued big time. She was shutting that high-speed traffic lane down. When she got finished only one person at a time would be allowed to use the Internet. Each keystroke would be monitored, effectively taking everyone back to before the horse and buggy days. Surely that would slow things down to a grinding halt. Who would want to wait until their third or fourth life for one second on the Internet?

"We got a call earlier," Officer Novell said over her thinking about all the damage she was going to do to the wide world of webbing. "Two male subjects were picked up tonight on the highway. They were stopped a mile before the rest stop for drinking and driving. We have them in custody."

Double Dare

His words brought her thoughts to a screeching halt. Instantly she and Phyllis snatched around at the same time to look at each other. Jesus have mercy! Or rather, Jesus had no mercy. They were getting creamed for this one when Frank and Joe got out of jail. Rolled back into view were those two caskets.

Officer Novell watched their faces change colors. Mona's turned a copper bronze, with a silverish hue, and Phyllis's turned a pearly bright pink. "Do either of you have a husband that could be described as wanting to kill you?" he heartily laughed.

Now that wasn't funny. They both had husbands who fit that description. Could he be a little more specific? They needed more to go on. Like, 'did either happen to mention how they wanted to kill them?' That might help. Frank had a look that could kill, and Joe was good with deathly words.

They walked into the highway patrol visitor center, with their heads bowed and very subdued, fearing the absolute worst. Before the final assault, the part where they would be asked if they wanted to post bail, would be their last chance to decide on how their fun should end. Starting all over, as in finding a new life… and husband, or really starting over—as hoping they might get a chance at a second life. Decisions, decisions. This was going to be a tough one.

"Have a seat here ladies," said Officer Novell. "We have some paperwork to wrap up before bringing out your husbands."

Mona looked over at Phyllis, now the color of a shiny nickel. "Did he just say—" her words thwarted by Officer Stayton placing the car keys in her hand.

It was a telling moment. The moment Phyllis used to jump up, catching on as Officer Stayton placed the keys in Mona's hand.

"Wait Mo. We're the ones supposed to be getting arrested!" she shouted indignantly, as if the officers were robbing her of the chance to be free from Joe's wrath. "This isn't fair," she carried on. "Why aren't they putting them cuffs on us and hauling us back there to toss in one of them cells!?!"

Mona didn't answer. She sat there frozen stiff watching their executioners head their way. Phyllis saw them too, and piped down the moment she did, seeing Joe taking those lethal steps towards her, mirrored in Mona's widened look of harrow.

"Oh Mo—Frank looks really mad," Phyllis said, only moving her tonsils.

"No, I think Joe looks madder. Look at the bottom of his arms. Looks like two bowling balls tied to his wrist."

"Oh God, do you think we should turn around and run," Phyllis asked, still only using her tonsil to speak.

"Maybe we should just try to jump that counter and go for someone's g—"

"—Hello Mona," Joe bitterly greeted her. "I know it was you who put Phyl up to this!"

Double Dare

Mona looked to Frank, pleading with her eyes that he defend her. But he only glared back.

"She did not put me up to nothing," Phyllis shouted at Joe, surprising the heck out of both Frank and Mona. Even Joe jumped when she spoke up.

"I can make my own decisions," Phyllis contended. "Plus, I begged you countless times to take me to see Hairspray! A whole year Joe," she screeched in his face, "and Mona finally was nice enough to take me!"

"What the devil," Joe mouthed aloud. "Come over here woman, so we can talk this out in private," he said pulling her off to the side.

The moment they moved away Frank spewed, "so how does a show end up in a brand new car you can't even drive Mo?"

"I can too drive that car," Mona argued back. "I just didn't want to drive it until I got more practice."

He started to argue with her, but that there was an argument he couldn't contest. Who could argue with a defense that made no sense?

They blamed, they shouted, and fought, accusing each of many things over the 95½ miles it took them to get home. For a minute Joe would try to hammer on Mona. Then Phyllis would hammer back at him, before he started cursing Frank's temperamental old Olds, blaming the radio that kept going in and out, and the dashboard lights that didn't work. No wonder he didn't notice his speed. The odometer didn't even work.

In the other car, the spanking hot brand new G37, Mona accused Frank of not being understanding, and then Frank slammed her by asking her to explain where she got the money.

'Ut oh.'

But she said she would talk about it when they got home, except at four in the morning they first got to slamming a sequence of doors—car doors, front doors, bedroom doors, and even kitchen cabinet doors.

Eventually she got around to explaining the money, powering him down almost instantly.

"When were you going to tell me this," was his final defense, to which she slammed that one down too.

"This account is over a year old, Frank" she said. "Have I ever once during that time given you reason to think I was acting different?" She didn't wait for him to answer, knowing he had no answer.

"No! I haven't! I even let you call me all sorts of fat slobs—"

"—hold up Mo," he said raising his hand. "That's not fair. I never ever called you a fat slob."

"Well...pretty close," she said. "Always accusing me of raiding the cabinets and surfing the Net sitting on my duff."

Chapter 11

"No Mo, Joe's really peeved about what happened," Phyllis said to another one of Mona's fantastic ideas.

She wanted to get them together to discuss a cruise to Africa. That being, sailing from America to Africa, something she just got off the phone from discussing with an incredulous tour operator.

"All Phyl—why don't you send Joe a nice little cutesy apology card and then come on over."

"No Mo, I'm telling you. Joe takes a while to get over things. For this one he's going to need another month or two to get over. You and Frank will have to coordinate this trip and go on your own."

"Phyl. Phyl. Phyl…I'm telling you," Mona baited her, using a voice she used many times before to get Phyllis to see things her way. "Just send him a nice little 'I'm sorry' greeting, right now while he's in there working. I bet you anything he's waiting for this cheer…and will be so surprised seeing it come from you."

As Phyllis mulled over this Mona baited her more, and with a piece of bait she was sure Phyllis couldn't resist. "You don't want some little hot-tottie to come along during this vulnerable moment he's in. It'll be his excuse Phyl—" Mona let her voice drag on, smiling deliciously wide.

It worked. Phyllis thought about this. Joe worked in an office full of sharp polished women. She often felt small around these women. Joe said he didn't care for any of them. He liked what he had at home, but this could be a moment when he changed his mind.

"But Mo, I don't know how to send a greeting card," she edged out, fearing another mishap as grand as the mishap she was about to apologize for. Unlike Mona, who was savvier with technology things, she stayed away from Joe's computer. That was his thing. When he wasn't glued to the plasma screen, she could count on seeing him in the den wearing the strange headgear playing computer games.

"It's easy!" Mona cheered her on. "Here, I'll walk you through the steps," scooting up to her desktop, excited about Phyllis so easily giving in. And Yae! They were almost a step away from the Mother Land.

Phyllis looked over at Joe's computer, daunting as it was, minding its business scrolling pictures of his favorite all-star players across the screen.

"No, I better not," she decided when Harrison and then Suggs panned across the screen. The last mishap really wasn't her fault, though he got angry with her still, but if she messed up his computer…woo…there was no telling how angry he might get. He could end up crushing her like one of the bone crushers floating across the screen.

"But, I'm going to help you Phyl. Don't worry. The Internet is not as scary as it seems. People say all those things just to keep people like you shut out," she said, having long since put aside suing IE over that Internet deal that went perfectly. "I'm transcending you into the 22nd century with the rest of us!" she told Phyllis.

Twenty minutes later she finally convinced Phyllis enough to at least move the mouse. It would get those creodonts off the screen she told her. "Now what do you see?" Mona asked.

Her next hope was that Joe didn't have his precious computer password protected. That would mean extra steps; steps that might involve her having to throw on clothes and pay Phyllis a visit.

But Joe didn't have a password on his computer. And why should he? Phyllis never touched it. She didn't even know how to use it.

An hour later and Phyllis was good and giddy. She had opened Internet Explorer (IE) and was on Yahoo's homepage setting up an email account.

"Oool wait," she exclaimed. "Flavor Flav is opening a new restaurant. I want to read this. Me and Joe met him once, while we were out to dinner," she excitedly clamored, telling on Joe and his gift to gab managing to impress even Flavor Flav.

"Okay Phyl—now here's what you do…" Mona said, ignoring the Joe spiel. What was new? Joe was a known braggart. He didn't know it, but it was one of the things Frank liked least about him.

She guided Phyllis to the free electronic greeting card site. "Look at the cards and select one you like," and she added coyly of course, "I would go with one of the more suggestive ones. You know how Joe is. He won't care for anything with balloons or flowers in it."

Phyllis followed her instructions, clicking on boxes until she found one she liked—a congenial enough greeting that would get the message across without being too suggestive, since she was sending it to his work, and wasn't that type person anyway.

"Boooorring," Mona snored when she saw the U & Me greeting.

"But Mo, I'm sending this to his job."

"No you're not," Mona yawned. "Joe is at his job, yes, but you are sending this to him…not his job."

That didn't make sense to Phyllis. He'd be opening this card sitting at his desk. "What if his boss is there, hanging over his shoulder and sees it…" she begged to understand.

"Oh, Joe's not stupid," Mona said. "He won't open it with people around."

That still didn't sound kosher, but Phyllis went on clicking and looking, a little excited to learn something new. She could easily get addicted to the Internet. No wonder why kids were hooked on it.

"Ooo! I think I have one here!" Mona sat up, having navigated to a riskier site while yawning through Phyllis's dry selections.

It was a striptease card, not so bad compared to the others. It was an appropriate apologetic sexy and humorous card all rolled in one. Phyllis was written all over this one. She started to guide her to putting an image of herself on the other end of the whip, but knew that would take way too long. She'd have to start with the convincing all over again.

She guided Phyllis to the site, and mercifully heard the words she waited to hear. "I like this one! Okay, so what do I do next?"

"Wait...I'm reading..."

Phyllis waited, bouncing in Joe's comfy cushiony chair, telling herself she was going to have to go out and buy one of these computers when she was done. Who could have ever guessed the Internet would be so much fun.

Nearly five hours after pulling up to the computer to contrive this apology, about thirty minutes before Joe was due home, one of her deepest regrets had been sent. It went with a whoosh!

"Joe's going to love it! I know him," Phyllis beamed, proud to learn something new. "And he's going to be so surprised—" —abruptly she interrupted herself, doing a 360- flip around in tone.

"Oh my God Mo! He's going to know I used his computer!"

"No he won't. Just close out of everything," and Mona guided her through the steps to close down and delete her history. So long as his system looked like it hadn't been touched, he'd have no reason to check folders to see if it had been.

"Whatever you do," Mona cautioned, "if he asks about how you sent the card, tell him I let you use my laptop when I stopped by..."

Chapter 12

Next day Mona was sitting at her desk, an ancient but durable antique piece of furniture her boss gave her as a parting gift, seriously working on that America to Africa cruise. Wearing her large Goldie Hawn specks and her typical wear—sweats, slippers, and wielding a mean hot cup of Colombian coffee and slave-a-day thoughts, she was intently scouting out an itinerary for this cruise when Phyllis called screaming.

"Wait...wait Phyl—calm down and tell me what's going on," Mona said, just about ready to scream too.

It took five minutes of panting, but finally Phyllis got it out. Joe had just called and said she sent a porn email to everyone at his company. Well, this wasn't exactly how the conversation went. Phyllis never got out the part of Joe first asking if she sent the email. Had she said no, this story just might have wrapped up there...provided Mona's America to Africa cruise never set sail.

Joe initially didn't even know Phyllis sent the email. All it said at the top was Dear Joe, and was signed your buttercakes, a pet name Joe infrequently called her. There was a little bit of a filler, the part that clued him in it sounded like Phyllis—the apology part where she and Mona came up with that one liner... 'thanks for rescuing us, we'll never do that again.'

But he closed out of the email, feeling a little strange, but sure Phyllis not only wouldn't have, but also couldn't have sent that email. She knew nothing about computers or email. A while back he tried to show her a few things, but saw she was hopeless...calling icons by pet names such the Saturn E, (for IE), and the peace ball, for the

Double Dare

button that powered on and off the PC. There was no way she could have taken as many steps as it'd taken to send out this email.

If anything, he figured one of his female stalkers were playing a nasty trick on him... coyly using his name and the pet nickname he called many women. That one-liner was the kicker though. No one but he, Frank, and the wives knew about that trip. Well, and Officers Novell and Stayton, and maybe a few at the precinct. But then they wouldn't have had anything to do with sending a card. It wasn't even funny, barely even cute, another reason why he felt so uneasy about it. It just had Phyllis's palms all over it.

What prompted him to call Phyllis was after his boss, Waldo Isadore, pulled him in the office. He walked in all ready to discuss a shipment of cameras, only to be slapped upside the head with that eerie email. Apparently there had been a link attached to the email now going viral, and most apparent according to hothead Waldo, the IT department had launched an all-out investigation and made one hair-raising revelation.

"Where were you at 3:39 today," Waldo asked, as if he hadn't heard him in one hair-raising conference call trying to convince a prospective client denser than him how essential their cameras were to its business. Waldo even paced by his door several times during that time, giving him the thumbs up.

"You know I was on a conference call with Zappo," Joe answered anyway.

"That's not what our records show," Waldo said, the last technical man on earth to know anything about technology. He didn't even dress the part, wearing the Washingtonian crisp white shirts and neckties always too tight.

"We just had a major breech," Waldo said, trying to straighten a tie that wouldn't budge, doing his best to look serious.

"IT thinks that email might've imbedded a virus carrying malicious spyware," he said, trying his best to paraphrase a sequence of words he knew little about.

"That email was sent from a personal Yahoo account belonging to Phyllis Witherspoon. And the IP address originated from the other half of this Phyllis Witherspoon—Joe Witherspoon."

"Do you know anything about this email?"

Joe jumped up out of the chair and dashed into his office, slamming the door behind him to dial Phyllis. Well, he started to call her, but then got to thinking… what if it was one of his stalkers? He didn't want to trip himself up. He was a smooth operator. Not no ordinary Joe Smoe. So he paced around for quite a few minutes as he thought about how he would come at Phyllis with this one…then he went ahead and called, but just to get her off the list of suspects as he tried to open the link looking for the real suspects.

He was sure something like this was far out of her league. Phyllis barely liked sex, so he knew without a doubt she had nothing to do with linking a porn party to a

Double Dare

greeting card. For cripes sake, she barely could turn on the damn computer.

"Did you just send a card over here," was the way Joe opened up with Phyllis.

She detected the hostility in his voice right away, and right away panicked. Oh God! She did something wrong. She was in trouble now. Mona managed to get her in trouble again. All these thoughts rained through her mind as she blurted, "no, Mona sent it!"

Phyllis didn't know it, but the confession was like music hitting Joe's ears. Mona could be considered a stalker. She wasn't his wife, and there was a love-hate relationship going on between the two of them. Crap like this she was always getting Phyllis caught up in. Always putting nonsense like this in her head, and then standing back to let Phyllis take the fall. Joe told Phyllis to cut ties with her. She was nothing but trouble.

So Joe went on to tell Waldo that it wasn't either him or his wife who sent the card, and that he believed he knew who was behind the prank. He then met with a colleague to take another look at this supposed porn party that had been sent in the link.

Chapter 13

But that wasn't all going on behind this one innocent email. After Phyllis had thrown Mona beneath the bus, and Joe was busy trying to figure how to throw Mona beneath another bus, Waldo and one Wilma Olgsby were engaged in a heated debate about the email.

"Joe has been slacking around here Waldo," Wilma fumed, making her eyes look like one of those rotating gunneries used in a many wars back in the day. Which speaking of a gunnery, Wilma looked something like a gun sergeant. Tall, square-shouldered, and a flat twin-cornered forehead she chose to advertise by wearing her hair combed away from her forehead in a frock of biblical curls, she had all the markings of an estranged bitter woman built to destroy the enemy. But the great nerve she'd take powdering her cheeks in red rouge. Every man, woman, and especially enemy, would take one look at her and credit her for the crushing defeat of free libraries across the country.

That's where Wilma came before coming to work for I-Technocon. She started as a reader and ended up as head librarian for the entire western half of the city. She was responsible for being one of the most brutal defenders of censorship. It was surprising there were any books in the libraries she manned and overran. She banned everything, and in addition to frightening away readers with those rosy cheeks and knots on her forehead, she ran her husband of fifteen years straight into an early-unmarked grave, too.

Double Dare

The Internet brought her regime in the library to a sizzling end, though it didn't stop the blushing warden from terrorizing other businesses.

I-Technocon loved her brassy grabbing men by the balls and turning them upside down to shake all the coins out of their pockets. They needed someone like this; someone who didn't want to hear nothing but coins falling out of people's pockets.

Thing about Wilma though, she grabbed all men by the balls. She hated men. With a passion, despite kind of looking like one. Put a hat on her head to cover the Sunday pressed curls, and snatch off the antique pearl earrings, and she could be a stand-in for Sam Jackson.

Without question, she hated Joe. He represented everything she hated about men. His philandering was at the top of her long list. She couldn't wait to get his balls in her grip, and now here the opportunity fell into her hardened chivalrous hands.

"I'm surprised you haven't done something about him long before now," she said to Waldo. And this was outside of the fact that Joe had ten years on her. She just got there. He waved and tried to smile at her once, but ever since she saw him as a sexual deviant.

Waldo wasn't so happy with Joe's performance either. Ever since he bought that home in the hills, he'd been aching to see him lose it. How dare Joe one up him like that. He knew he had just bought a home in the valley, and he goes on and slap that one on him.

Never ever outshine the boss. It was the easiest way to buy an early retirement plan. Waldo promised Wilma he would look more into the matter, in effect locking horns with one of the most notorious women known for stomping on a lemon and grinding it into a substance unrecognized even as pulp.

Word soon filtered down to Joe, who really started getting in Phyllis's ear about it.

"We could lose the house Phyl—" he paced in front of his gorgeous 72" inch flat screen. "This could be it," his eyes nervously danced around like two puppets on a string.

And Phyllis transmitted his every word right back to Mona.

"Mo, we could lose the house. We should've never done this. Oh my God Mo—if we lose the house I don't know where we'd go."

Mona didn't take any of this flippantly. She feared what might happen to Joe and Phyllis. Plus, Frank had gotten on her about it, too.

"How dare you do something like that. Fix it!," he seethed. Joe got on his nerves about a lot of things, but they had been friends for years. Plus, Joe was his boss. Well, he wasn't really his boss, but he had helped him get in the company. If Joe lost his job, then there might go his job as well.

So the America to Africa plan had to be put on the back burner. She had a problem to fix, which the irony here was...this was right up her alley. Turning crappy situations into moneymaking ventures—the crux of her business. How she grew that nice fat account that had Frank's eyes doing cartwheels and doughnuts. All she needed was to come up with the perfect strategy.

She scoured the Internet all morning after getting Phyllis's call, backtracking her steps to first figure out what in the hell went wrong. How had Phyllis managed to attach a link to the one innocent email she checked before guiding her to it? She since figured out how the email went viral around Joe's company. She shouldn't have led Phyllis through cutting and pasting Joe's email address into the email. She ended up copying the entire address field—Joe's and the All-Staff address.

But what was done, was done. She now had to get Waldo and that Wilma person off Joe's back, and of course, get Frank off her back, too. He swore if Joe and Phyllis lost that house, their marriage would be over as well. All of them would pay dearly for this deed if it wasn't fixed.

Chapter 14

Bingo! Mona hooked onto another idea.

She thought of it after learning what the hoopla was behind the so-called pornographic link. She had to forward the greeting card to herself to see the link, never figuring out how the link attached to the card in the first place, but there was the porn.

Unbelievable. Two residents at a senior home had thrown a 100th birthday party. About five senior men, and a dozen or so women, all in their 90's and over, were having the time of their life cheering on these two residents celebrating their birthday.

These two women were in the center of a dance floor, dancing, holding on to their walkers albeit, but nude it appeared. It was hard to tell. Mona had to watch the clip several times before she figured out they were dressed in a costume. But boy, to see those airbags swinging, and them trying to crouch wearing very embellished thongs, had to be the most priceless piece of hilarity she had yet to see.

How dare anyone would seek to stamp out fun like this. Two women get to this age and could still move the way they did, deserved to honor their years above ground however they saw fit. So, the plan Mona came up with, therefore was birthed out of a little rage.

Mona did her homework. She visited the senior home and met the two superstars, surprised to learn that it was them who accidentally sent the video to an online greeting card site thinking the site was like one of them 'uTube things'.

"Yeah, my great-gran told me to do it. She said it probably was going to be a hit," laughed the younger woman, by a day to the other woman. Her name was Foxy. And Foxy, like Mona, had a dream of performing on stage.

"Ha! Ha!" she proudly laughed when Mona told her the video indeed had gone viral. "All these years and I finally made it big time to the TV!"

Mona didn't have the heart to tell her uTube wasn't that kind of TV, and that, like Phyllis, she somehow screwed things up and sent the video to a greeting card site that published the video in an electronic animated format that now was receiving a lot of bad flak. Not that Foxy would care, no more than shrugging it off and saying something like, 'maybe we'll figure it out next time…' but she recognized the dynamic spirit in the woman, and in her friend Sin, too. And yes, Sin clarified for Mona how she now spelled her name. No longer Cynthia, she started going by Sin, spelled S-I-N, after doing her first dance 85 years ago.

She almost forgot her mission after getting caught up in Sin's and Foxy's energy, only wishing they'd leave enough for her to stash in her bra, closet to her heart, so she could get to it when needed. The women could give a rats behind if the video was offensive.

"Don't watch it. Turn your head," Foxy laughed.

"I would have done it without that dern bodysuit," fussed Sin. "I couldn't move like I wanted to," she said.

"I know," Mona chimed in, just to see them abuzz with all this edifying energy. "But some are concerned about children seeing—"

"—Children? Where's chillen?" Sin asked, looking around as if she was looking for children in the room to see what they looked like.

"Small children," Mona answered, demonstrating by hand, raising it to about the height of a small child.

Sin sucked her teeth and fanned the air, rolling her eyes and turning her head. Another resident sitting nearby was about to pitch into the conversation when Sin turned back around to face Mona.

"They don't know how they got here. When we was youngins, we knew all that stuff."

"Child," Foxy added on, "there ain't many chances in life. Every one of 'em you see, you su'posed to grab! Like this!" and she lurched out to grab a piece of air.

Mona loved these two. They were the oldest in the home, still with vim in them. It reminded of her high school, when everyone wanted to hang around those with that certain magnetic pull. That's how it was here. Although Sin and Foxy did the most talking, they weren't without an audience. A small crowd gathered around, which included a younger woman, only 88-years old, named Ms. Lily.

Ms. Lily, though, sat a little off to the side. But it was hard to see her as sitting off to the side with so many sitting around the magnets. She was just sitting a little further away, which too could've been attributed to her visitor…her son, one Lester Lord. That porn video lured Mr. Lord in for visit.

"Mother, how do you feel," Lester was asking, the part Mona overheard.

"Fine," Ms. Lily feebly answered as Mona headed to the door.

"Don't worry, we're going to get you out of here," Lester said.

Mona stopped and started digging in her purse, of course pretending to be searching for something at the bottom of it.

Back to the reception station Lester went, pulling aside a man working at the front desk. "I need to speak to Pam," he demanded.

"But she isn't in today," reasoned the front desk receptionist.

"Well call her damn it. I will not leave my mother in here for another night to endure this type of abuse!"

"No one's being—"

"—I want Pam in here this instance!"

"But—"

"—Now!"

But while Lester patted his foot as the nervous receptionist scrambled behind the desk trying to figure out how to call Pam on her day off, Mona moseyed over to the other end of the long desk. She pulled aside a worker who overheard the exchange as well.

"What's the story on that one? I'd like to have a word with him," she said to a grateful worker who'd been wishing ever since Ms. Lily arrived that a miracle would arrive and take this Lester son off their hands.

"He's always been like that," warned the worker. "The most miserable man I've ever met, while Lily is as sweet as can be."

"Too bad she can't do anything about that jerk now," Mona said, as her best yet idea swelled in her belly, soon about to be born.

"Oh, she would if she heard him," said the worker. "She's hard of hearing…probably isn't wearing her hearing aid, so she can't hear him. But if she could, she'd surely say something. That's why he's not as loud as he would be if she wasn't around."

"Oh really," Mona deviously smiled.

She waited until Lester stormed off, after razing Pam's ear for all of thirty minutes. The woman couldn't have gotten out more than hello…if that. The man blazed her for thirty minutes without taking a breath.

After he left Mona asked the worker to get Ms. Lily's hearing aid. She had something to put in her ear, and wanted to be sure she put all of it in there.

A worker dashed upstairs and brought back Ms. Lily's hearing aid… even helped her put it in.

"Hello Ms. Lily. My name is Mona. You don't know me, but I'm looking into the matter about the party you all held for your friends Foxy and Sin. Did you enjoy yourself?"

"Haaa Ha!" Ms. Lily squealed so loud she startled Mona. "Did I enjoy myself," she belted out too. "We always have fun at our parties. Not a one of 'em has ever been a let down."

Mona smiled and came in for the kill. "Well, did you know your son is trying to wipe this place out and have it closed down. He's going to have you moved to a new home."

"What!?!" Poor Ms. Lily's eyes stretched open, and her hand started quivering. Desperately she looked over at the receptionist, back to tending to his work.

"Danny," she called out to him.

Danny looked up and rushed around the desk when he saw her look.

"Danny, please get Lester on a phone for me—"

"—Okay, sure Ms. Lily," Danny said, hesitating to query Mona in an absence of words.

But Mona only smiled and winked. "I think Lester deserves to learn how to live and enjoy life. How about you?"

Evidently he felt the same, returning to the desk to retrieve a phone for Ms. Lily to have a word with her son, Lester Lord.

Chapter 15

And that's how double-dare came to be. While Ms. Lily and her gang of friends, Foxy and Sin included, planned to go toe-to-toe with Lester, Mona challenged Phyllis to get back at those two on Joe's back as well.

But as usual, Phyllis hesitated at first. "I don't know about this one Mo…"

"Don't you see? We don't have a choice. Frank is threatening to divorce me if you guys lose the house. And where will you and Joe live with our relationship beneath rocks?"

Phyllis saw her point then. Well, almost…

"It's fine that Ms. Lily can test her son like that," Phyllis said, referring to Ms. Lily's plan to demand that Lester bring her to her home, the one she by power-of-attorney handed over to him, every Saturday to enjoy a full day with her and her friends lounging by, of all places, the pool. If he missed one day, or didn't sit and join in with them and whatever they were talking about, she was taking back the house and giving it to a charity. And if he so much as retaliated against the home where she was staying, she was taking back the house and rewriting her will to turn over to the senior home for their legal defense. If she hadn't taught him better before, she was going to grow him up straight this time. Like Foxy said, and she believed, she had to take every chance she saw, and grab it.

"But how can we stop Waldo from firing Joe?"

"Well…" and Mona got good and excited on this part, rubbing her hands together already ready to go to work. "I was thinking about giving Waldo a piece of my mind."

"Huh?" Phyllis dropped her lower lip. How would giving Waldo a piece of her mind do any good?

"That's right," Mona went on. "While I was out and about window shopping today, I learned Waldo doesn't like unhappy clients. Angry clients are a threat not only to I-Techno-rabbits—"

"—I-Technocon," Phyllis corrected, now sure Mona probably hadn't thought this all the way through.

"Yes, Techno-whatever they call themselves," Mona waved away. "The point is, I learned a little secret that Waldo doesn't know," she grinned, shirking her eyes.

"What? What did you learn?"

"Well, I'm glad you finally thought to ask." And Mona clasped her hand and rocked in her chair, far too pleased with her detective work to sit still.

"I happened to run across two little birdies talking today," she started in a fairytale fashion Phyllis had to appreciate, even if the apprehension on her face didn't show she did.

"One little birdie said to the other little birdie…I can't believe they sold us all these licenses that are about as useless as chewing gum is to a newborn," Mona paraphrased in her best kiddie-like voice. "And then the other birdie said to the first little birdie, 'I'm reporting them to the BBB if we don't get our money back. This is fraud!'"

This wasn't exactly a chance run-in either. She had to dig these unhappy clients up, in a daylong Internet search digging up I-Technocon's brag list. The camera store was listed near to the bottom, which being a small business and at the very bottom of the list and all, she naturally assumed they were small fry, which they were, and knew good and well I-Technocon had probably gotten over on them, which they had.

Phyllis just looked. Aside from knowing little about IT, she knew next to nothing about business. Mona may as well have been talking to a seal beneath water in a language seals didn't speak.

"Phyl—our husbands work for crooks. Hundreds of licenses those spineless wheedles sold to companies and they don't even care," Mona went on, this time in her regular voice. "The company makes cameras Phyl—cameras that people buy to take pictures of their children at birthday parties and graduations, and at special events like reunions. Why in the hell would they need a security device in a product like a damn basic camera!?!"

Phyllis shrugged. She was lost at the point when Mona first started talking about giving Waldo a piece of her mind. How this tied into that she hadn't a clue.

"Welp, guess what?"

Slowly Phyllis started shaking her head, just about ready to beg Mona not to go through with her less than brilliant plan. "Please…no Mo…please don't do it."

"Yes Phyl, we are," Mona said ignoring Phyllis's protests. "I am going right up to I-Ain't-Techno and giving Mr. Wally World a nice big piece of my mind," and Mona hopped up out of the chair. "Like spla-dow!" she shouted, tickled by Phyllis's awestruck expression.

"Come on Phyl—it'll all work out fine. I promise."

"But…but…" Phyllis could barely speak. Mona had no limit. She would push by any barrier. She must have been the child who failed that glass cliff test, countless of times. God help her if she continued to stay friends with her visually ungifted friend.

"But…what if Joe sees you? This is his boss. They work in the same office," she said in what came out as a desperate spineless plea.

"Oh that…yeah…I've got that all figured out too. I already got my get-up. It's back there in my room," she nodded towards her bedroom. "I'm going as a dude," she said matter-of-factly.

Phyllis's mouth popped wide open, wider than her eyes were popped open. "A what?"

"A dude." Mona demonstrated, strolling around like the cool thuggish dudes did, throwing one arm behind her back, dipping, be-bopping, and nodding her head and whatnot.

"Oh God Mo—I think you've really lost it," Phyllis muttered. There was no way Mona could pull this off. She could hide behind all the neckties, dips, and strolls, and moustaches every male she'd ever seen strutted in, and still, wasn't nothing going to hide those hips!

Phyllis couldn't help it. She burst out laughing. Both of their lives precariously hanging on by a slim thread and she laughed so hard she couldn't stand up straight. There were no words, except for these few.

She looked at Mona and said, "I double-dare you."

Chapter 16

Mona got dressed, after Frank cleared the house, taking her time applying a little shadow to make like hair on her face. Thanks to a wig studio coming out with the most incredible pieces since afros came back in style, she found a short neat afro that matched her brows. She didn't want to overdo it. Actually, it was okay if ole Wally started trying to wonder her true sex. It might make him lose his train of thought while she blasted the hell out of him.

Getting rid of her breast was a little problematic. Phyllis came over for that part, and for the hips, which were a larger problem. Phyllis was right there. It took a lot of muscle to wrap a whole sheet around her body in a way that would make her look straight up and down, like a normal dude with a face as small as hers. Most men didn't have small faces and large bottoms. Just wasn't the norm.

But Phyllis went to work, with her lips tucked in holding safety pins, and using her arms to get the sheet good and tight around her mid-section to even out her waistline with her hips.

"Hold still," Phyllis said, fastening the sheet at the back by duct tape. "Wait a minute…" she said grabbing the stapler. "Let me staple this piece just in case..."

Mona stood in front of the mirror, nodding her head, admiring Phyllis's handiwork. "This looks good Phyl—I now look straight up and down."

Phyllis nodded approvingly too, satisfied with her work. "Just make sure you don't lose Frank's shoes if you have to run out of there. You know they could be used as evidence," she laughed.

Mona looked down at her feet. "Yeah, I think you're right. How about we duct tape these to my ankles?"

"But how's that—"

"—look," and Mona started to sit on the bed but found out she couldn't bend like normal. She had to fall on her stomach and let Phyllis secure the shoes to her ankles that way. She started taping up one shoe, starting from sole nearest the heel, running the tape up and around the shoe and ankle. It was a quick fix. The hard part was rolling her over to help her stand up.

"Come on Mo—you've got to practice squats in this thing, or else your cover might get blown."

"Like this," Mona asked, extending her arms and bending at the knees.

"No, like this," and Phyllis demonstrated by karate chopping her in the stomach and pushing her forward.

"Ooo," Mona moaned. "I didn't feel a thing. Do it again, but hurry…" She only had a few minutes left before she needed to be in the car and driving. Her meeting with Waldo was schedule for 10am, and it was already almost 9:30.

Phyllis did it again. "Now lean side to side a little. It might loosen up the tightness some."

Mona leaned, still feeling a little stiff, but pressed for time she had to get going. "Now how do I look," Mona said facing Phyllis, trying on her serious face.

Double Dare

"Ugh...well you kind of remind me of that guy who played in 8-mile..." Phyllis said, wishing she could think of someone who looked more like a businessman than a rapper. But if she thought on it any longer she might end up telling Mona the truth. She looked like she was on her way to prison for a long, long time.

"Who? Never mind," Mona hadn't seen the movie, so there was no point in even trying to figure whom that person was. Plus, she was getting a little nervous, and started to sweat beneath all the draping. She now wanted to get this over and done with. If she went by the script, which she knew by heart since it was an issue she took issue with, then it wouldn't matter whom she looked like. She could look like the legendary Tupac for all that would matter, so long as Joe, and thus Frank got to keep their jobs.

She drove to I-Technocon, about a twenty-minute drive from her house, when along the way she heard a pop, or maybe it was a tear. Something felt like it was coming undone, which by the time she reached I-Technocon the bandaging felt as if it had shifted some. She could feel a little wobble when she walked. But she just hiked up the pants, careful not to let the tape around the shoes show, and put a little stroll in her strut as she walked across the parking lot. Too bad Phyllis wasn't with her. She would've asked how she looked from behind. For some reason she felt like one of the Telly Tubbies looked...from behind.

Got inside, signed in, and was given directions to Waldo's office. She had only a minute to spare, which gave her no time to stop by a bathroom to adjust the increasing slippage. And then too, which bathroom would she slip into?

So she kept moving, reaching for the belt as if she was going for a concealed weapon. Got on the elevator, and off the elevator, to bump into of all people, Joe!

She almost said it too. 'Hey, Joe!' But thank God she remembered why she was there and who she was perpetrating to be.

Joe though stopped, and looked hard at her. She could read the look on his face. He was trying to place where he'd seen a similar face. He squinted, turned away, and turned back around as if he figured out exactly whom he was thinking of. But before he could speak she gave him a look that took the words out of his mouth, especially when she said, "we got a problem here? There a problem!?!"

Now the regular ordinary Joe out on the street may have taken her up on this threat, but this Joe was at work, and treading very thin ice as it would be. One sudden move out of him and either or way, his job was as good as gone…or so he must've reasoned.

Chapter 17

Slippage, smearing moustache, queer voice and all, and Waldo turned out to be a piece of dark sweet chocolate cake. She walked in his office, dipping and be-bopping like she practiced, and got him good soon as she tossed the contract she sort of bribed off the two birdies, on his desk. Fla-dow!

As expected, Waldo was a mite of a man. He had the biceps of a washed up linebacker, and hands like a bricklayer, but a pale chump from start to finish.

"You think you're slick, don't you?" she be-bopped in place, standing in front of his desk scaring him good, though probably because she was using her regular voice.

She let his thoughts jangling around for a bit, trying to figure out what was wrong with her voice, and if maybe she, him, or it was in the wrong office.

"Ugh...excuse me Mr.," and his eyes scrambled over papers scattered in front of him, searching for this offbeat unprofessional businessman's name.

"Harry," Mona said real ugly-like. "And just look at you. You didn't give two damns about meeting me on this did you? You think I'm some rooty-poot kid you can kick around, selling me junk you knew I couldn't use...not answering my calls...but spending my money like it's really yours."

Waldo stood up, but Mona sat him back down. "Don't you dare touch that phone. Touch that phone and it'll be the last call you ever make." And real stiff legged, only because she was trying to keep the sheets from wobbling loose, she closed the door.

He was still grasping at pinecones trying to put all these two-and-twos together. For one, he and Larry White, the actual owner of the camera store, were scheduled to meet. Not this Harry Masood person. And two, this person didn't look like no Masood he ever saw. Masood's didn't wear afros. And was that red nail polish he was looking at?

"Listen here Wally Beaver," she pointing dead in his face…two lovely manicured red nails clearly visible that she paid not two bits of attention to.

"I sell cameras, bud. Cameras that take damn good pictures of regular stuff. People, cars, animals, and the sky for Christ's sake. But you sold me, and at least eighteen other idiots, licenses that don't go with our business model.

Now, I see what you're doing. You're like everyone else out here trying to shake loose a buck from a tree that don't have no leaves. But I have kids to feed too. I've got to eat Wally. Which means, if I don't get my money back, and get my money back real soon, me and eighteen of your other idiots will be running you in to the BBB. And you do know who the BBB is don't you?"

"But you…" and he cleared his throat, "I mean, your company signed the contract."

"Wally, I can read. I know we signed on that there dotted line. But Wally, you know damn well you had a lot of cooked up fine print in that contract. That's why it's up to you to be the expert. You supposed to know that a regular dime camera store don't need nothing in its camera encrypted. Just name one way, right here, right now, how this is gonna fit my business."

Waldo stared at the rolled up piece of paper on his desk, as if he first was trying to guess what was in it, while actually trying to come up one reason. Anything would do. Even something generic would do, except nothing came to him. He couldn't fish up one clue that could clue him in as to why a dime store camera store would need high-tech security cameras.

"See! You can't name a one. And guess what Wally? Neither can me and the other eighteen idiots."

A few tense seconds got between the exchange as they faced off with each other. Her glaring at him, and him staring back at her.

"Look, we don't have no magic crystal balls—"

"—You don't have no what," Mona hissed, leaning over and placing all four knuckles down on his desk. "Am I hearing you right Wally? Did you say you don't have no crystal ball?"

"That's what I said," Waldo said, swallowing hard.

"Wally, listen at this," and Mona raised up, bringing Waldo's eyes up waiting on her to pull out the weapon. "If I don't get my money back, and get my doe back fairly soon, you and all your friends around here gonna wished one of ya'll did have a crystal ball on the day I decide to come rolling back through here!"

And she turned to walk away, almost forgetting the major line she was to pitch she got so worked up in her client's defense.

"And one more thing Wally," she said catching herself in that turn, "if Joe out there lose his job, I'm still going to the BBB about all this fraud you keepin' up in here. I got 'cho ass on camera buddy!"

Chapter 18

They celebrated, and celebrated, and celebrated some more—her, Phyllis, Joe, and Frank. The thing was, Waldo tried to call her bluff by calling the camera store and speaking to the owner. But Mona wasn't no slouch on the job. She had done her homework. Larry told Waldo that he indeed did hire Harry Masood to help him work on the unnecessary and unused licenses.

Waldo though, asked for a description of Harry, in a sly way however, which Mona had her tracks covered there too. She told the owner beforehand that Harry Masood was her colleague. He handled all the face-offs. The owner didn't know what Masood looked like, but whatever he looked like, he would be back in rare form if Waldo didn't meet his demands.

This was where Joe came in, which Mona brought him in unwittingly, at the celebration he and Frank just as unwittingly participated in.

"Yeah Joe," Mona slipped in as they were playing a hand of Gin Rummy. "I heard about I-Techno selling all these fraudulent licenses to businesses like free Willy-Nilly."

"How'd you hear that," Joe looked up, stunned. Phyllis looked over at Mona too, only slightly more bewildered than Joe.

"I was in the camera store when I overheard them talking. You know that's what I do. I'm sure Frank over here…my do or die partner has told you this," and she encouraged Frank on by giving his leg a nudge, beneath the table of course.

"Sshew…" Frank sighed, shaking his head, thinking back on all the loot Mona managed to stash. He wasn't like Joe, so he never told him the size of all the numbers he saw, but he hadn't seen Mona out of the same two eyes since.

"Man…" and Frank drug man out. "All I have to say is, if you need consulting advice, see Mo!" And that's all the juice, Frank not being as big of a show-off talker, he added to the syrup.

"Yeah…Waldo got all bummed out about that one," Joe said sadly shaking his head, before chuckling to himself in what Mona took as an afterthought. "…That camera store sent some hit-man up to the job. He really shook Waldo up…whoever he was," Joe splashed on.

"But Joe, this is where you come in," Mona baited him like she often did Phyllis. "If you can get the store to buy from I-Tech what they really need, I bet Waldo would see you in a different light." She was speaking about that husky after midnight grief Wilma was dousing on him, which she had plans for the unloved madam as well. That was phase two, the part that would bring on the fun with a mean vengeance.

Joe didn't answer right away, but she read on his face he was thinking it was great idea…something he hadn't thought of, but wished he had.

"The thing is," Joe contemplated, searching his small brain for how he could make something like this work, "only Hollywood can use the stuff we make."

Boy! Did he ever not say a mouthful? Half of the technology out there was little more than passing entertainment. But while that big buzzword was out there, let her not stop the show.

"I have a client I was talking to about the cameras… you know, after overhearing the conversation that day in the store, who I'm going to meet with in a couple of weeks. Maybe if you have some spare stuff that's piling up in your return inventory, I might be able to sell it to them," Mona baited him on.

"Awl shucks, I have hundreds of all kinds of camera devices," Joe boasted, so typical of him when he was happiest.

"Oh, really? Why don't you—"

"—Phyl—why don't you hang out with Mo more? Watch how she works it. And whatever you do, learn how to send an email!"

They howled, as she called bingo for the second or third time. This was it. Phyllis was now locked in, all owing to her agreeable husband's greedy bragging disposition. Who said there was a dying art to swaying unpopular opinion? If no one said those words, then she was. Joe, without any arm-twisting, proved that there was.

Chapter 19

Mona and Phyllis sat in a stake-out car playing the Odd Couple in a really theatrical version of CSI, Streets of San Francisco, Cops, Law and Order, Murder She Wrote, and all the rest all mixed up and bunched up together. In fact, Phyllis climbed in the car, Mona's G37, looking like she was doing Angela Lansbury. She naturally had the pudgy cheeks, and the buggy round eyes, although Mona would never say this. It might hurt her feelings, like she hurt her feelings after she figured out who the character was in that 8-mile flick. Phifer who? Chile Please! But had it not been for the headscarf and large fashion shades she picked up off a grocery store rack, Phyllis would've been a shoe-in for that Lansbury role. She was good. She even wore the exact trench coat that woman used to wear on set.

"Do you think she'll take the bait," Phyllis asked, like her natural jumpy self. A role she didn't need any extra lessons to improve on. It could be 100-degrees outside and someone say, 'I hear it's going to snow,' and Phyllis would go into character, without even waiting for the sentence to finish.

"We'll see," Mona said. There was always plan two through as high as anyone could count. Mona planned to make sure of that. This was her dream.

"Joe said she's a big woman. What if she tries to fight us?"

"Will you calm down," Mona turned and told her. "We haven't even hit the road yet. We're just going to watch her take the flyer off her windshield."

That's all there was to it. Wilma was going to walk out of I-Technocon, see the flyer on her windshield, get perturbed about seeing trash on her car, cry to herself about insensitive people violating her crummy public space, but like any used-to-be ex-warden of a library system would, she was going to read it anyway, and hopefully…the part Mona wanted to see, stuff it in her purse planning to follow up on the elaborately worded Ad she spent a whole 9 days concocting.

"Joe says when we get back he's taking us to Spain," Phyllis said, trying her best to stay calm and positive. Picturing a beautiful ending had to be the way to go.

"Oh, look. Here she comes," Mona said, sitting up straight in her seat as Phyllis slid down in hers.

"What's going on…is she reading it… What's she doing," Phyllis rattled like a chilly beaver.

"Open your eyes and find out," Mona rattled back excitedly. "She hasn't even gotten to her car yet."

But Phyllis couldn't force herself to sit up like Mona. That was too bold to attempt. She barely could open her eyes, even sliding down in the seat. That was Mona's role, a character tough enough to watch Wilma approach her car, and as anticipated snatch the flyer off her windshield, scoffing as she did, but reading still.

"Bingo!" Mona quietly cheered, almost bringing Phyllis to sit straight up in the seat. "Hold still," Mona warned, reaching over with the backhand to keep Phyllis in her downward position. "She's too close."

Wilma opened her car door, pausing briefly to scan around, and seeing nothing out of order she hopped in her car—a beat up old Imperial Chrysler that should have stopped working the year after Chrysler sold that model.

"What's she doing now?" Phyllis wanted to know, but Mona couldn't answer right away, on account of Wilma driving right by the car and looking directly at her. Mona, though, pretended to be looking around her, despite catching the woman's hostile glare, as if asking, 'did you put this trash on my windshield?'

"Okay, the coast is clear," Mona said after Wilma had pulled off the parking lot.

"Phyllis slowly sat up, sighing loudly, as if they had the woman tied up and in the trunk. "Gosh Mo…" she heaved again. "I don't know if I want to go through with this thing or not…"

"Awl, don't worry. Soon as we hit the road, you'll probably be the very one who won't want to turn back. Joe will have to go to Spain all by his lonesome."

The thing about it was, Mona penciled in the grunt work for herself. All Phyllis had to do was coordinate with Bobby, a young kid who flirted with them every time they were out buying beer for the guys. They connected a while back, the day he had the nerve to card them, telling them it was company policy that he card everyone who looked 30 and under. He'd been flattering them ever since; that being ever since he stopped stuttering after trying to figure out how old someone would have to be, born in the 60's.

The flattering led to frequent chats about him studying film, and how he wanted to take part in this huge film festival, but was short on cash…and ideas.

Right away, this guy was all of Mona's speed. He spoke her language, and was a serious artsy kid not hung up on life's trivial matters that didn't center on and revolve around theatre and film.

Mona interacted with him a lot, visiting the store for more than the guy's beer runs. She knew where he lived—in a run-down trailer park with a mother who drank whiskey and reminded her 'a lot' of a woman who used to be pretty, before she gave up on life. Mona didn't want to see the same thing happen to Bobby, as he was a handsome son…looking 'a lot' like a young Travolta, and plus, he harbored her dream too.

So, she promised him, and even helped him on few school projects he worked on at the arts university he attended part-time. They had been at this film thing for a while, and so now here was their big break.

Timing couldn't have been more perfect. The film fest was little more than a week away, the biggest fest in the country. It drew participants from every crack, crevice and hole. The richest and the poorest got in on it. Fees were steep, so of course, no one wanted to lose. Bobby himself always said, 'he wanted to earn more than that typical 'thank you for entering' condolence all 60-70 thousand applicants received'…more or less for just taking the time to pay the entrance fee. This thing wasn't cheap. That meager $150 to enter was beans in a bland stew compared to the labor involved to gather resources and materials.

Mona explained what she came up with, and Bobby loved it from the byline: Grabbing a Man by the Balls, Turning Him Upside and Making Him Smile. A play for Wilma was on the next line, but that was irrelevant to Bobby. It only meant something to Mona…and Wilma.

In the same 9 days she spent on the script, Bobby used 7½ of those days running ragged to pull the other essentials of the film project together. Storyboarding, finding cheap actors, nailing down locales…a lot here was involved. But then this too was his dream, so it was hardly a bother, especially not when 75-grand and a movie deal also sat on the line.

All Phyllis had to do was READ…and follow the script, while Mona…and Bobby did the labor-intensive work. Oh wait…Phyllis did play a major hand in getting things rolling.

Phyllis supplied the cameras. Joe let her walk out of the house with a box of those cool cameras; the ones with the built-in cool security devices that I-Technocon had been pushing off on unsuspecting mom and pop stores that no one but Hollywood could use. There was only one caveat to this. He expected 'them' to sell the cameras. 'They' had to agree to this, after telling him it was the reason for the trip. He would've never fallen for a film project, and most certainly would've keeled over twice had he heard Wilma was involved.

Double Dare

But these little creatures were awesome. No bigger than a thumbtack, they could be worn in bracelets, necklaces, and hair bows, or anything that a thumbtack could be adhered to. They had to have them. They were perfect for this project.

And still, Mona had the bigger task. Her job was the thread that would sew the entire project up the seam. She had to first lure Wilma to that old theatre no one in dozens of years ever visited, and essentially kidnap her.

"Okay Phyl—you ready? Got everything in place?" Mona asked one final time before they would meet up the following day.

"Yes Mo," Phyllis promised. "You know there's no way Bobby will mess this up. Not with the way he's been crying about doing this film all year!"

Mona pulled away leaving Phyllis standing at the foot of her ample home knowing between her and the voluble nature of films, there was going to be phuck-ups. A script, no matter how well financed, or low-budgeted as theirs was, ever followed the rough draft. It wasn't supposed to. This was the true art in making art, where the other big splash fell in for Mona. She planned to have a blast, even if she pulled off, away from Phyllis's house penciling in the worst.

Chapter 20

She kissed Frank that morning, feebly whispering in his ear, "wish me luck."

He responded in kind, like always, "enjoy your trip. Knock 'em dead tiger!"

Frank, like Joe, thought they were on a mission to sell cameras—to fly out to Hollywood and talk well-versed men out of hundreds of thousands of dollars to buy I-Technocon's fancy security cameras. Talk about dreaming? Obviously they weren't the only ones with above average dreams.

Truth was, she left out of the house that morning very nervous. The first day would be the strangest. If anything could go wrong, this would be the day for it. Plus, it was slated to be the longest…and hairiest. She knew it without a shred of doubt. And why? Well…she planned it this way.

She arrived at the Hobb Knobb, the place where she worked on occasions, the same place Frank scoffed about for her burning up gas to get there, the place she only opened on three other occasions that year, and propped open the doors to let some of the musty air out. Smelled like old buttered popcorn and grubby muddy carpets in there.

But it was starting out to be a pretty day, perhaps a good sign, seeing a pallid sun warming the nakedness around the theatre just enough to eat up some of the smell crawling out of the theatre.

| Double Dare

She doubted that Wilma would turn her nose up at the moldy stuffy odor though, not being an ex-librarian warden and all. But she didn't want to be sniffing mold all morning, waiting for Phyllis first, and then Wilma to show up. They could pull up and find her passed out dead, and then what? Wilma would remain in her comfy little box a pent up mean rattlesnake. Phyllis would go crazy. And poor Bobby. She hurried up and opened those doors on the thought of poor Bobby.

There really wasn't much else to do after that, since Wilma would be the only patron buying 'a' ticket that day. So she sat in the booth, kicked her feet up on the ledge, and tried to read a book around mocking birds singing. That was the real beauty about Hobb Knobb many missed. Its classical singing birds. They seemed to love to sing over moving silence, which there was plenty of that around Hobb Knobb. Wasn't a residence or business, or anything but farmland for a 3-mile radius all around the theatre. So these mocking birds took up residence, using the area as a meeting ground it seemed. It's when they got feistiest with the singing, getting so loud that they sometimes could be irritating, especially like now when she was trying to read and rehearse in her mind how to handle all the 'what ifs' for things that surely were going to go wrong.

All she could hear were those darn mocking birds, reminding her of when Hobb Knobb was a popular spooky spot. Back in the 70's it used to be the city's number-one hang out for Fright Night and Halloween, owing to its castle-like architecture. A William the IVth designed it, in the late 1800's for an elite circle he used to entertain with operas and such. But when his opera social circle died or moved away, the theatre fell into the hands of many artisans with many ideas for the old theatre.

For a while after the operas moved out, the theatre stayed vacant, gathering cobwebs and dust until an art collector came along and started hanging famous work in the building. But he died of pneumonia, though not before willing over his collection, to include ownership of the theatre, to a brother. That unnamed brother was undermined by another brother, who had big ideas for the theatre, resulting in a bloody feud, and the theatre next turning into a speakeasy.

Hobb Knobb, briefly renamed, The Bourbon House brought the theatre up in popularity. Sheldon, its new owner, housed any man's tamest to wildest dreams in there. From moonshine to sex, to anything above and below film, to even fresh produce sold in the wee dewy mornings while rogue night partiers slept. Everyone wanted to say they had been in there once. It was a badge of honor to be a part prohibition, however this delinquency badge could be fit in. But unfortunately the Bourbon wasn't around long. March 29, 1929, a year after the takeover, one of the bloodiest shoot-outs in popular history closed down the Bourbon for good.

A saxophone player got his hands on the theatre a few years later, turning over a jazz club for a short spell, restoring the Hobb Knobb's name before closing down to the next reign of control.

Many of these upheavals occurred prior to Hobb Knobb settling into what it was originally meant to be, a theatre for fine film, even if during the 70's locals saw it as a place to host the most elaborate haunted houses, charging exuberant fees and drawing in large crowds.

But not anymore. People weren't interested in the theatre anymore, even on that one day of the year. Only tourists as far away as Japan respected its place in history, opening its doors to cinema before any other theatre in the country.

Mona pulled her legs off the ledge and sat up when she saw Phyllis pulling up in front of the theatre and hopping out of her car.

Here we go, she thought, rushing out of the booth and out of the theatre breaking Phyllis's stretched grin and fantastic story on its way.

"Park around back Phyl! Remember, there can't be any cars out front!"

"Oh yeah," Phyllis remembered, scurrying back in her car, and looking left and right and all behind for signs of traffic. There was none. Wasn't a single car on the parking lot because there was nothing within a 3-mile radius all around the theatre, almost the way it used to be when first built.

The most traffic Mona ever saw in her time at the theatre was during Halloween, and during the early 80's when a strip mall was built. But that was leveled during the Dot.com boom; no business cropping up since. That's what made the theatre such a gem to hang on to. There was no rent, barely any taxes owing on it, and the utility bill too was next to zero. It was just a shell of a theatre that happened to be able to still play movies on its ancient cameras.

"I'm sorry about that Mo—" Phyllis sheepishly grinned, appearing from around back to take up her assigned post—to stand at the window and act like a customer.

"Do you have your car keys," Mona asked, apology accepted when she first asked Phyllis to play the role.

Phyllis opened her hobo bag and peering through another pair of off-the-rack large shadowy spectacles peeked inside. "Yep, there in here," she said taking in a deep breath as she looked up at Mona giddy in the face. "Do you think she'll fall for it?"

"I sure hope so," Mona said starting to worry a bit. The beginning was the bloodline of the entire plot. But she worked hard on that bait. She hoped Wilma would go for it.

"I just ho—"

"—Let's talk positive stuff," Mona interrupted. She was starting to feel jittery. All this hoping would only make her feel even more jittery.

"Yeah, you're right. No since—"

"—sssh! She's pulling up on the lot now."

"Oh God…oh Lord…Oh geez…this is it…oh God…I should have used the bathroom before I left home."

Double Dare

"You sure should've Phyl—because a Thunder Cat is headed this way and it's time to take this show out on the road!"

Mona scooted on the stool and sat up straight. "So ma'am," she said in a loud clear voice, "if you'd like, you can use our facilities. Just come on inside. It's the last door on the right," Mona said, motioning for Phyllis to step aside.

Phyllis didn't answer. She adjusted the large cheap shades, and fidgeted with her hobo bag, zipping it and unzipping before briskly scurrying inside the theatre.

"Hello ma'am," Mona politely greeted the prudent Wilma taking a giant step up to the window, pulling a scrolled up paper out of her bag as she stepped.

"How may I help you?"

"I'm here to purchase..." and Wilma looked down to uncrumple the badgered piece of paper in her hand. "...This was left on my windshield the other day," she said instead, and she said it with this big disgusted chip on her shoulder, as if accusing Mona of smutting up her old beat up windshield.

"I would like to purchase 20 tickets," she finished.

Gulp. Twenty-tickets!?! Why? And for who? She had no friends. No one liked her. And that meant absolutely everyone. She was a bitter old ex-warden librarian out to ruin every man's career based on her deep hatred of a man she fifteen years ago already buried. She killed off many dreams, just about single-handedly.

But more so than all who hated Wilma, and sure she hadn't printed 20 tickets. She doubted if there were even twenty seats in the theatre. The last she counted there were ten in the balcony, and maybe... one, two, three, she quickly counted in her head the rows of seats on the main floor. Okay, so maybe there were twenty seats, but she hadn't printed twenty tickets. Damn it... just to think she was starting off unprepared gave her little hope for what lay ahead. She should've known this woman was showing up with more than the hooks and cranes on her forehead.

She had no choice. She had to jump off script.

"Wow, you're planning on filling our house," Mona smiled as if saran wrap was holding the lower half of her face in place. "You just about sold out this show."

Great thinking...she murmured as she pretended to be looking in a drawer; a drawer filled with nothing but rusty paperclips and dust. She lifted her eyes off the dust to find Wilma glaring at her, staring at her as if she stole her lunch.

"I think you've sold out this show," she said with the onion smile. "But I have an idea," she quickly added before Wilma could purse her lips to speak. Popping the top off a ballpoint pen she wrote twenty in the right hand corner of her ticket...circling several laps around the number.

Wilma looked down at the ticket she slid beneath the glass window, as if she had spit on it, and scoffed. "If you're all sold out, then how will this assure me, and my nineteen guests that we will all have seats!?!"

"Hobb Knobb is a very prestigious theatre," Mona replied. "We pride ourselves on knowing each one of our guests. Trust me, there will be enough seats for you and every one of your guests."

Wilma seemed to eat up that reply, although she tried to peer behind and around Mona, as if she was looking for something.

"Do you accept major credit cards?"

"Actually, we do," Mona said, whipping out a credit card machine. That part she had prepared for, even if she somewhat expected the irritable woman to whip out a post-dated check. That didn't happen, but almost.

Wilma whipped out a first generation AMEX card. The card was so old she thought it was her social security card. Of course it didn't have a magnetic strip on the back, which had Mona stalling to remember how to handle a card without the strip.

"You'll have to type it in," Wilma sneered, lifting her pointy snout as if she smelled something putrid in her near vicinity.

"Thanks," Mona said, though beneath her breath she muttered bitch.

One ancient credit card accepted and the receipt spitting out, it was almost that time, hurrying Mona's heart, making her hands tremble some waiting to tear the paper away from the machine. Wilma probably thought it was her though. She was used to making a lot of people tremble.

More jittery than anticipated, she slid the phony receipt beneath the slit in the window, while fondling the coil that would release the shade. All on her mind was hurrying up and closing the theatre so she could get out and enjoy some of that fresh air she could no longer hear the mocking birds singing in.

"Don't I need to sign some—"

—and she accidentally jerked on the coil bringing the shade straight from the ceiling of the booth down between them with a flapping thud.

Quickly she jerked the coil again, raising the shade lopsided. "I'm sorry about that," she clumsily grinned. "We need to have that fix—"

"—is there somewhere I'm supposed to sign for the tickets," Wilma breathed nosily, with the patience of chowing down hyena.

"Oh no," Mona lied, remembering something she once heard in a grocery store. "Under $50 there's no need." And then, as if there was any more room to venture further off script she added, "we have cameras that are as good as a signature."

Wilma heard her, but she acted like she hadn't. All I-Technos were cued by the word camera. "This is a strange place," she said instead, stepping back to look up at the building. Probably looking for bullet holes legend to be imbedded in the walls from that early bloody battle. But the ones she should've been looking for were ones left in more recent times…from that rogue family she hailed from.

Double Dare

The warden didn't have her fooled, stirring up all those bans on books, proclaiming to be the righteous of goodness. She may have no longer dealt with her family, ousted from all societies due to her morbid fascination of good and evil, but her ass hailed from a rough clan remembered not too fondly in the 80's as terrorizing local farmers shopping in the mall with all that gangsta activity. Pearls aside, apples rarely fall that far from the tree.

Wilma started to turn away but was stopped by a straggling thought. "What's the refund policy like?" she bitterly asked.

With her hand back on that coil, as Wilma would be the very last customer, she quickly rattled off "…full refunds! We offer full refunds, no questions asked to any customer who wants their money back!"

Obviously appalled by Mona's odd behavior she turned away, uneasily, and idled back to her car parked about five feet behind her. Funny, she had locked the door, so she had to open her purse to retrieve her keys. She also had to stick the key in the lock since there was no remote opener.

Mona watched through the closed shades. All she could hope was that Phyllis didn't pop out of nowhere yelling for the woman to stop.

Wilma started the car, turning the ignition with a little more gust than newer cars required, and placed one hand on the wheel and extended her arm to place the other hand on the passenger seat, to complete the rest of her due diligence safely operating this rather old vehicle. As if her neck hurt, she turned around to make sure the coast was clear. All clear she proceeded to back up.

POP! The sound was so explosive it made Mona jump, almost to the roof of the booth, five feet above her. She expected maybe a little hiss, but not a loud pop echoing on like a gunshot. The sound must have made Phyllis jump too because she heard a commotion in the back of the theatre. Sounded like boxes falling.

Casually though, Mona pretended she was busy closing the booth, though anxiously waiting for Wilma to ask her help. She heard the car door creak open and it bang close, pursued by her Mary Jane pumps walking over asphalt to the back of the car.

"What's she doing Mo?" Phyllis asked sticking her head inside the booth's side door.

"I don't know...stay out of sight," Mona whispered. "Come out when I flicker the light switch."

Several minutes later, after Mona imagined Wilma trying to use her cell phone, she heard the tap on the window. But instead of peeking beneath the shade, she stepped outside, into the open morning pastel sunlight, and scrumptious fresh air.

"Is everything okay?" Mona asked meeting a more contrite Wilma by the car.

"I was wondering if I might be able to use your phone... perhaps if there's a pay phone inside?"

Perhaps, you might... Mona laughed to herself, if there was a phone inside that worked.

Double Dare

"Oh, this old theatre doesn't have pay phones, but you're more than welcome to use mines in the booth," she said, fully back on script.

"I really appreciate it," Wilma said, following Mona into the theatre. "I just can't seem to get a signal on my phone," she more like mumbled to herself.

"No problem. Help yourself," and Mona opened the booth and gestured Wilma inside, letting her head drop thinking a ton of things. Of course Wilma couldn't get reception on her phone, which had less to do with the fact few mobile devices got reception in that area. That old hand-held Motorola she almost had to hold with both hands, Mona was surprised it got service anywhere.

"Hello! Hello!" Mona heard seconds later, followed by Wilma desperately tapping buttons trying to get a dial tone. It was a simple fix. The phone needed to be plugged into the right jack…though nothing Wilma would know, or find in the short time she'd be there.

"Is there another phone around here somewhere," Wilma came out of the booth demanding. "That one in there isn't working!"

"Oh no, that's the only phone I know of out here," Mona idly dragged out. "Who are you trying to call?" she asked, just as idly picking up the phone Wilma had seconds ago slammed down, to check out things for herself, for Wilma's viewing pleasure of course.

"Gosh, you're right," she announced after several attempts, all to no avail.

123

"I just don't understand it...why no phones around here work," Wilma spewed, suddenly taking in Mona standing there. "Do you have a phone!?!"

"No, I'm a herpetologist," Mona said blank face, dressed like how she thought a spiritualist would dress. The phony nose earring, dungaree waist-high jacket, flouncy flowery skirt, striped knee-hi socks, and Birkenstocks. And oh, she wore a large fake red rose in her hair.

From there Mona delved into her act, wanting to kick her heels up with everything going so well.

"You need a lift anywhere?" Mona asked, reaching inside the booth for the last of her belongings—a 20-pound rucksack. "I'm on my way home...my shift just ended...you can hitch a ride with me if you want. Won't cost ya' nothing."

Wilma looked around. There wasn't a car on the lot. There in fact, for three miles out, wasn't anything but nature's rawest resources alive and thriving; the sky, trees, and farms, which for Wilma dressed in the Mary Jane pumps and Sunday hairdo, was going to make for a nice hike trying to hoof it across Knowles farm, something Mona promptly informed her of.

"You want to be careful hiking into town. There are three wolves in that barn that the farmer keeps on the loose. It's all private property outside of that gate you drove in."

Mona read it in her eyes. She was desperate. Her walkie-talkie wasn't picking up a signal, and there were no working phones nearby, one of the features that made the theatre as haunting, and unattractive in the same. Actually, Knowles did have a phone, but first she had to cross the wolves, which of course, was no such thing. But even if she chose not to believe her, and tried to seek help from Knowles, she might find herself waiting until the harvest season opened before her knock at the door was answered. Her final resort was something else Mona already calculated. She could try driving on the flat.

Thoroughly disgusted she tried to do just that. She stormed away and hopped back in her car, bouncing down in the seat she was so enraged, and tried to turn over the car. Nothing. Mona almost laughed out loud. She could turn that ignition as hard and as angry as she wanted, but she was going nowhere without any gas. While she was inside the booth trying to make that call, Phyllis drained her gas tank. And she must have sucked that bad boy bone dry because the car wouldn't even sputter.

This was Mona's cue to Phyllis, flickering the light as she closed the theatre. They walked out at the same time, spryly chatting about the script...their blunders and goof-ups, and where they adlibbed.

"Do you think she'll follow us?"

"What other choices does she have?"

Phyllis started to look back, stopped by Mona. "Don't turn around. Herpetologists don't care about stranded people.

"Excuse me..." Wilma called after them, about half way across the parking lot.

125

Chapter 21

"Don't worry," Mona said to Wilma, looking so out of place up against her and Phyllis dressed like twin herpetologists. The only difference in their dress was Phyllis wore a yellow rose in her hair, and she wore it to the right.

"...Lots of people who come out here bum rides. You'll be in town in no time... ooo look, here comes a ride now," Mona said, casually sticking her thumb out as if she was born a herpetologist.

She was familiar with the area however. No one traveled this road, ever, and especially not coming from the direction the car was traveling in. They were standing at a dead end, something like thumbing a ride in a cul-de sac where there was only one house in the center of the circle, and no one lived in the house.

Going by the script the driver of the car should've been Bobby, but after a quick squint, Phyllis knew it wasn't Bobby. She knew what car she rented, and this old-mobile certainly wasn't it.

"Mo-Mo-," Phyllis tried tapping her arm, trying to tell her it wasn't Bobby, and to put her thumb away, but it was too late. The car, a model older than the thing Wilma drove, slowed and came to stop directly within Mona's line of vision.

Instantly she spun around to look at Phyllis, first wondering how she managed to rent a booby-trap, and secondly to note it wasn't Bobby inside.

Double Dare

"Hop in ladies," grinned the driver, a funny-looking young man obviously dressed in drag; wig and a fake mustache. Also, prominently visible at a small distance was his many missing teeth, detectable through an evil sneer. Everything about him spelled deliverance.

"You go on fella," Mona said to the driver, trying to keep her cool and appear hip. "We are ladies here, and we ladies don't ride in any hoop-mobiles."

The driver threw the gear in park and hopped out of the car, one foot in, the other out. "Git on in here, I say! You know ain't nothing coming from back that way," he laughed. "I won't hurt ya'! Now git on in here!"

Mona and Phyllis exchanged looks. They never saw Wilma's expression, because they were too worried themselves to look.

"What? I gotta' come over there and give you gals a shove or what?"

Mona almost lost her cool as she shouted, "Get out of here or I'm ca—"

—And she didn't get to finish. The toothless man pulled out a shotgun and had it aimed right at them. "I said git in this here car, now!"

The three of them crept towards the car and in single file started climbing into the back seat.

"You, the big mouth one," he said throwing his head towards Mona. "You sit up here with me."

So much for fun. This wasn't exactly what Mona had in mind. It certainly wasn't anywhere in the script. She remembered every letter. She wrote it. Bobby was supposed to be here. Phyllis promised he would.

But she had read a lot of true crime books about things just like this happening. Just play into the villain's ego and things might turn out fine. Staying cool was somewhere in the serial killer handbook too.

First thing she did was start looking around for clues. But the car was so old she could even tell the make and model. She would guess a Plymouth, but it could just as well have been a collection of many old cars assembled into one. The dashboard was missing. Stuffed inside were heaps of rotten paper and oddities she tried hard not to commit to memory. Beneath her feet, was another thing she tried to keep her eyes off of because was nothing but black asphalt down there. And bedspreads had been thrown over the seats to count as upholstery.

"Why you don't want to ride with Jimmy here," the snaggle-tooth stranger laughed. "I'm a good boy."

At this point she was also trying to breathe without taking in the sweet sickening scent. It smelled as if Jimmy hadn't bathed in a month.

"You hear me talkin' to ya!?!"

Before Jimmy pulled out the shotgun again she decided to say something. "Ugh…hi…" she said staring straight ahead, speaking very robotic. "Please let us out at the next town."

"You a pretty lil brown piece of sugar," Jimmy said, ignoring her. "Why, I bet you got you a mommy and a daddy, huh?"

Cringing inside Mona nodded she did.

"You scared of 'ole Jimmy?"

Out of her peripheral view she could see Jimmy taking his eyes off the road to look at her. He also had to be driving about 5-miles an hour, not that the car probably could go much faster. She again shook her head in the affirmative.

"Why you scared of 'ole Jimmy. Jimmy ain't never hurt a fly." And then out of the blue, startling her to jump since she hadn't heard anything, he yanked around and yelled, "shut that sniffling up back there! Ya'll actin' like I'm some kinda killer! Jimmy ain't no killer! But I can be if you keep makin' me mad!"

So, this was what it really felt like to be with a serial killer, just when she thought to glance down at the door handle. She didn't want to leave Phyllis, or Wilma behind, but maybe they might follow her lead when she bailed out of the car.

But there was no door handle. A round hole where the door handle used to be took its place. She tried to concentrate and look harder, but was afraid to turn her head and get Jimmy more riled. When she saw the town appearing in the distance, she regained hope and starting praying. Maybe he really was a good guy and would live up to his word and let them go.

Chapter 22

Normally, and on the worst weathered day, it took her no more than thirty minutes to get to the theatre. She lived in the next city over, on the other side of a village that separated her home from the theatre. It took her twenty-nine minutes to reach the village; basically an extension of Knowles Farm made up of a farmer's market, an abandoned police station, and several well-preserved cottages that used to function as Bed and Breakfasts. This was the farm's business center, where mostly, in recent times, people who lived outside the village, like in the city where she lived, drove to buy real fresh whole foods. But only on Saturdays.

On rare occasions she might drive by and catch a gracefully aging centurion idly rocking in a swing on one of the cottage's wooden porches, but that was rare, especially midweek when the abandoned village took on a charming fairytale look reminiscent of the many festive community socials once held there; smoke-outs traditionally held for Memorials Day and the 4th, and a big Polka dance held right before Thanksgiving.

Well, the minute it should've taken Jimmy to reach the farmer's market, took him a whole thirty minutes. And when he finally did reach it, and the three of them, make that four to include him, saw a sheriff's car parked outside of the farmer's market, she thought her prayer had been answered. She sighed silently, closed her eyes briefly…just to properly thank the Lord, and opened them to find he decided to cruise on by the village.

Double Dare

The gasps behind her could not be missed. Phyllis totally lost it. She started twisting and turning, and kicking and screaming like a mad woman. And really, who could blame her? But that was the moment when Mona realized something wasn't right. Phyllis was in the back seat having a lily black cow, and Jimmy acted like a Cello was in the back seat playing. Actually, that was incorrect. She looked in his eyes and actually saw a cello playing.

Mona turned around and got up on her knees so that she could reach Phyllis. The car was that old she could do this. It was actually one those cars with a bench-type seat up front.

"Phyl! Phyl!" Mona said, hoping to catch her eye while Wilma sat crunched over in the corner furthest away from Phyllis, as if she might have scabies or something. "Look at me Phyl!"

It worked. Phyllis found her voice, albeit through strained red eyes no longer protected by the large cheap shades. During her flight to fright the glasses had slipped down over lips.

"Do you want to get out of this alive," Mona said, trying to do an amber warning light improvisation. "Now calm down, please," and this time she flashed her eyes, to suddenly see Wilma trying to discreetly use her walkie-talkie.

"And you, put that away!" she hissed, snatching the radio out of her hand to give her the same flashing, pulsating warning lights. "Are you trying to commit suicide with this thing?"

Slowly she turned back around and looked at what she now recognized as a petrified Jimmy.

"You might want to thank me for that later," she said before rolling her eyes and turning away to stare at seemingly the same trees passing by like a dozen times each.

Finally, well over an hour later they made it to the outskirts of the farm town. They were coming up over a hill that would put them within sight of the city; a sight all of them, to include Jimmy and the griping old mobile, breathed nosily to see.

The car pulled onto Kohl's parking lot, clanking and rocking, coughing huge white balls of smoke to make one ceremonial clank the moment it left the black top road for a graveled parking lot. So make it five entities glad to finally reach the city. She could almost hear Phyllis and Wilma lean forward as they thanked their Lords. This was it. It was then or never, she heard them thinking.

Jimmy pulled the honker into a parking spot at the far end of the shopping center, furthest away from the stores' doors, and killed the engine. He hopped out of the car, all bad like, when he saw 'the operative.'

Right away Mona turned around, kneeling in the seat again. "Okay, stay calm and we'll be okay. Don't make any dumb moves because none of us in this car can outrun a speeding bullet," she said, seeing Phyllis staring at just who she saw. Bobby—the operative.

Double Dare

But big bad Wilma wasn't buying the stay calm. For the first time she spoke, and the woman had not a tear nor fear in her eye. "We could've taken that guy!"

"Yeah, but this isn't about looking out for just ourselves. We want all three of us to walk away together," Mona spat back.

Wilma looked at her as if she was wearing three heads. "I don't know if you know this or not young lady, but that is a kid. And that kid is wearing his mother's wig. So, as soon as one of them opens this door, I will be walking away from this, with or without you!"

Well!!!

Except Bobby was now on the scene. Wilma had lost her say in the matter. Bobby, as the old saying goes, was the Real McCoy!

"All right, this is the way it's gone' down here from here on out," Bobby said hopping into the driver's seat, wearing beastly long sideburns and rocking a long flighty scarf rich kids making a political statement typically wore. He smelled good too. It smelled like he bathed in Giorgio, mercifully overpowering Jimmy's sweaty odor.

"We gonna need a lot more loot to finish this job," Bobby said as Jimmy, who Mona now decided had to be one of his friends he was studying fine arts with, slid in the car beside her.

Jimmy snatched off the wig, signaling something was not quite right, as Bobby went on talking about this loot they needed to finish the job.

"The way I see it, we gonna need at least two more G's!" Bobby said, swinging around in the seat to look at Wilma. "Old lady, how much you got?"

"Young man, I do not carry that kind of cash on—"

"—Old lady, I didn't ask nothing about no cash. You got credit right? Everybody old as you got a credit card. You carrying one on them cards aren't you?"

"No, she doesn't have any money," Mona quickly answered, cutting her eye over at Bobby, but tucking in her lips trying not to laugh.

"A'ight. A'ight. Then here's what we gotta do. We gotta rob a bank," and he sat back in this attitude that said his hands were tied. He had no other choice.

Right away Wilma leaned forward. "Here young man. Take my AMEX. There's two grand on it. Take it please!" and she tossed that old social security card over the front seat.

Slowly picking up the card, turning up his nose and mouth as he did, he scowled, "what the hell is this?" He turned it over, holding it as if he was handling a soiled diaper and said, "this thing don't even have no strip on the back! How we gonna get money off this thing?" And back around he snatched. "You tryin' to get us caught old lady?"

"Tell the clerk to type in the numbers," Wilma dryly said as if she was tired of playing the childish games.

"Oh I see," Bobby said yanking his head in Wilma's direction as if no one but Mona could see him. "This one bored."

Double Dare

Bobby adjusted himself in the seat, stomping down on the gas pedal to crank up the car as he prepared to turn it on. "Yeah, we got us a real bored one," and he turned the ignition so hard that it scratched the engine, making a dull grating sound.

"Ugh…I don't think this car will make it through a robbery," Mona helpfully offered, throwing her eyes in the direction of the rental Phyllis had rented just for this trip.

"Oh yeah, I see your point. Good lookin' out lil sis. We gonna squeeze you off a nice lil cherry when this lil operation is all over."

Bobby started to yank open the door but Mona stopped him again. "Ugh, what's your name?"

"Putn'tame," he said. "You know the game. You ain't supposed to know your kidnappers name."

"Well Putn'tame, if you open these doors, we are all going to do our very best to escape," and she hoisted her eyes backwards in Wilma's direction.

Bobby quickly looked back and saw Wilma sitting back there just a gritting her teeth and juggling her jaws. He thought for a minute and looked over at Jimmy gazing out the window as if he was waiting for the car to turn over so that Bobby could drop him off at the next corner.

"Mo D!" Bobby said all un-rapperish like. "Help me get these girls and the old lady out of here, one by one," he emphasized, "so there be none of this business of trying to run away."

Jimmy sighed and started to open the door when he realized there was no handle. He turned to Bobby looking like he and Wilma were on the same page and said rather blandly, "yo Bo-bo, the name is Jimmy. Now Bo-bo will you please open my door so I can get out of this piece of junk."

Soon as both Jimmy and Bobby were out of the car Wilma immediately leaned forward and snapped at Mona, "is this your idea of—"

—but she didn't get to finish her argument.

Chapter 23

No cameras could visibly be seen rolling, but it sure seemed as if they were already showing on the silver screen—headed straight for a front row seat at the next Oscars. Without training Bobby and Jimmy could be a shoe-in for Starsky & Hutch, except instead of two leather jackets, denim wearing tough beat cops, they were two educated nerds dressed in a crude mix of Fonzorella herpetologist apparels.

Tired of the prickly wig, Jimmy had pulled off the stache, deciding to play out the rest of his skit going as himself—a nerdy white biology kid dressed in high-water khakis, a wrinkled b-b-balled crewneck double-knit top, and no-frill sneakers dug out from beneath a pile of dollar items at the thrift store. Add a pair of binocular lens secured to his face by a rubber band, and there completed one nerdy look.

He didn't say any of this, but his attitude said he didn't like something about the way the skit was going. He was ready to bail, but Bobby trying to play it cool, wanting this gig more than Jesus wanted redemption, begged him to hang in there. Things were about to look up…thus this resulting in an old-fashioned high quality Bonnie and Clyde bank robbery, nowhere written in the script.

The two nerdy kids following a rough sketch how a bank robbery should go down, based on watching the movie Bonnie and Clyde, pulled out of Kohl's parking lot with the two mid-aged motley dressing housewives parodying herpetologists, and one angry ex-warden librarian mad about the proverbial bracelets uglifying her mannish wrists.

"Did you get the masks," Jimmy quizzed Bobby, still a little grumpy about the matter.

Bobby reached in his pocket and pulled out a Kohls bag. "They're in there," he said, tossing the bag over to Jimmy. "Picked them up while I was waiting on you," he said.

"Awl dude," Jimmy moaned pulling two black wool ski masks out of the bag. "We're gonna burn up in this crap. Besides, the Barrow gang didn't wear masks!"

"Yeah…but this is almost a hundred years later. We are doing it how they would do it if they were in this day and age," Bobby intelligently argued back as he calmly drove up a major artery lined with banks.

"Dude, I don't know where you've been, but in this day and age, Bonnie and Clyde would be in their hotel wiping out banks, with a machine gun pointed at the door for anyone who stopped by to ask questions," Jimmy huffed, nosily throwing the masks to the floor.

Mona wanted to look over at Phyllis, to see how she was taking this little spat. She hadn't mentioned anything to her about a robbery, because it wasn't in the script, which made her curious to see what page her thoughts might be on. As for her thoughts, they were a praying this wasn't too real.

"Hey, guess who I saw in Kohls," Bobby said all gaily, and again way off script.

"God," Jimmy blandly answered.

"Awl dude, come on…lighten up. I saw Marty. I—"

Jimmy snatched around, alarm zapping across his wiry face as he looked Bobby. "—I sure as hell hope you didn't say anything!"

"He already kno—"

"—All for Christ crying out loud!" Jimmy groaned in agony, rubbing and shaking head and throwing it back against the headrest.

Suddenly the mention of Marty put Jimmy in a new mood. He leaned forward, looking out of the window and pointed. "Let's do that bank over there," he said.

Bobby looked over there, on the other side of the wide highway, which meant doing a U-turn. "Why that one," he asked as he hit the turn signal to switch lanes.

"'Cause, when I first moved here they charged me a late fee, and wouldn't reverse it."

"Yeah, all banks are creodonts," Bobby agreed. "They are worse than Bonnie and Clyde. They took my mom's house and gave it to one of their brats!"

Jimmy swung his head around to look at Bobby again. "They did what!?! Which one? Which one of these crooks took your mom's house!?!"

"Orchard," Bobby said.

Jimmy looked around, trying to see if he could find a bank that had that name, as Bobby moved into the lane to make a U-turn.

"I can't see no Orchard. So how about we go on and hit that one that hit me up for that late charge? They probably are cousins or best friends or something anyway," Jimmy gave in, sitting back.

Bobby made the U-turn, but missed the turn that would have put him on the parking lot of the bank Jimmy pointed out. "Shit, I missed it," he said, looking around trying to figure out a way to swing back.

Jimmy lifted up again. "Yeah, that's how they get you. They make their entrances hard to get to, so you can't easily get to them, to stop them from charging all these ridiculous fees."

"Hey man, how about if we just go with that one over there," Bobby asked, pulling onto a lonesome plot of newly developed land where Prudential sat by itself.

Jimmy shrugged. "Yeah, I guess. It really doesn't matter. All of them are the same."

"Good, because I was trying to avoid doing any hold-ups in areas where a lot of people are around. That's the easiest way for someone to get hurt," Bobby said before reaching between his legs to bring up an Uzi that looked very real.

"Hey! Watch how you handle that thing man!" Jimmy yelped, jumping to get out of the way of Bobby's swing.

"Awl man, it don't—" and Bobby played with his eyes, skipping over a part he wanted to say…but didn't. He kept it at, "it don't have no magazine in it… yet!"

Double Dare

That time Mona did pan a glance over in Wilma and Phyllis's direction. Guns weren't in the script either. But both of them looked away, in different directions, giving off different vibes. Wilma stared off to the right, giving the world she stared at a really hostile glare, while Phyllis seemed to be doing just the opposite. She had no idea how far off script they were...not until both Bobby and Jimmy grabbed the wool masks, pulled them over their heads, and hopped out of the car.

Only then she took note and spoke up. "Hey, what's going on, what are they doing?"

But Mona didn't answer. At this point she was on Broadway, and unscripted, going for broke watching the two nerdy dean's listed kids, rocking to a funky Benny and the Jets beat, pull on double doors to a major bank, in broad U.S. daylight, almost looking like two wooly swordfish with their heads popped out of water, to go inside and do only the Lord knew what.

Bobby walked in the bank carrying the Uzi like a guitar, after politely holding the door for Jimmy to walk ahead of him. He even did a little Sugar Ray dance at the door, for their viewing amusement.

"Look, I've had enough," Wilma sighed, shifting in the corner where she had wedged herself. "I find this entire skit really offensive and ask you to have them stop this now."

"Shut up you meanie!" Phyllis spat back, across Mona who leaned back to let her have her say. This was the first time she vocalized her disposition. "They just need more money to teach you a lesson about kindness."

Okay...the plan just about foiled in 20 divisions, Phyllis goes on, and true, innocently revives the script. Wilma didn't have a comeback. She merely turned back to hostilely face the window.

"Ugh, Tootie," —Phyllis's covert name, "but what if they do try to tie us to this bank robbery," and Mona laid special stress the words bank robbery, "saying all of us were in co-hoots?"

"Oh, they're not really—"

—And before Phyllis could say the words, out dashed the notorious Bonnie and Clyde, waving up in the air two bloated white bags with dollar symbols printed boldly on the bag.

Both nervously fumbled opening the door, and jumped inside to which Bobby started yelling, "Go! Go!"

"You're driving Bo-Bo!" Jimmy yelled back, when suddenly a pink and pale gutsy man came flying out of the bank fanning his hand and yelling, "Stop! Stop! Give us back with our money!"

Recklessly looking back, Bobby peeled out of the parking space and whipped the car around on two and a half wheels to face an exit sign.

Chapter 24

They took a pit-stop break ten minutes away on the other side of the city, about ten miles away from the airport. Uncle John's gas station was where they stopped. It was an out of shape service station that probably since its opening never had more than one or two customers a day. And none of those one or two customers were there to buy gas. They were there for the same reasons they were there. To use the outdoor facilities.

They parked around back out of view of any needy customer desperate enough to stop by and want to use its bathroom too. With all four doors open, something like photographed in the illusive photos taken by the Barrow gang, they got out to stretch their legs.

"Come on you three," Bobby beamed, "get out of there and stretch those legs."

Slowly the three of them climbed out of the car. Wilma first, as she seemed most desperate to get in that outhouse.

"Now, just because I'm taking off your pretty bracelets, don't get no great big librarian ideas and think you can run off," Bobby laughed in Wilma's face. "I'm a tenth generation Jesse Owens. I will beat you to that street before you set your first foot down."

Wilma just glared at him, clutching her purse beneath her arm, about to walk off.

Bobby chuckled more. "I bet you didn't know that… that Jesse Owens part," he laughed in Wilma's face as he snipped off the bracelets.

"And oh," he said, snatching the purse from under her arm. "Let me hold on to this for you. I know how you smart ones are. Don't want you getting no bright ideas, thinking about holding us up while you sit on the jon chatting up your girlfriends," he said, shucking his shoulders and laughing as she walked off.

But Wilma didn't protest. She hurried to the potty-room as they excitedly clamored around Bobby the moment Wilma closed the potty room door.

Grin stretch ear to ear, Bobby held up both moneybags to pose for the first picture.

"Oh my gosh, Bobby," Phyllis crooned, leaning into him as if he really was the handsome Clyde, running one hand down his small chest and kicking up a heel to gleam into the lens for the second pose.

"You like that didn't you," Bobby beamed, holding his head up high to stick a stick in his mouth, making like it was a cigar. Snap. That picture was taken too.

"Come on over here and get in on this too," he motioned to Mona, filled so full of emotion she wanted to break down and cry.

"Yeah, but how'd ya'll like the way that manager came running out the bank," Jimmy joined in beaming too. "That was really cool. I hope the camera got a close up of that shot!"

"Well, let's just see what all we have in these money bags," Mona ruggedly laughed opening one of the dollar sign bags and poking her nose inside.

The look on her face when she lifted up was one of absolute horror, which… snap! Jimmy laughed hard on that picture taken.

"Bobby, this is filled with real cash—"

—snap. Another picture captured her reaching in the bag to bring up a fist full of twenties.

"They gave you real cash," Phyllis asked, sticking her nose inside the bag too.

"It was the deal," Bobby big-daddyishly exclaimed. "A bag full of credit cards wouldn't have come off right," he said, taking the bag from Mona and tossing it back in the car. "The thing now is, how are we going to deal with this miserable tart you two are trying to happy-fy?"

"I hate to say this but I think we're going to have to sedate her like you suggested earlier…at least until we get to the studio," Mona said. She couldn't think of any other way to get Wilma to soften up and go along with the maddening skit.

"Awl, come on…before the old battleax gets off the pot," Jimmy said, dancing around and grabbing the Uzi to throw his foot up on the sideboard of the car. "I want this pose," which for good measure he started to light the end of a Benjamin to smoke.

Bobby smacked the lighter out of his hand. "Man, are you crazy?"

"Wait, here," Phyllis jumped in, throwing an arm around Jimmy's neck. "Then take this one," and they leaned in towards each other for a long simulated kiss. Jimmy had his lips puckered, looking at Phyllis, while she puckered her lips sort of sideways, so she could keep an eye on the camera.

"Wow," Jimmy said, stepping back to stare off in amazement. "This really does feel great."

"Yeah, and you doubted me," Bobby hit him with just as Wilma emerged from the potty-room.

Snap. Jimmy discreetly snapped her picture. She wasn't smiling, but looked somewhat relieved. Phyllis, though, catching Jimmy snap the picture came up with an idea of her own.

"Aren't you happy Willie!" and she merrily sprang into Wilma's arms, smacking her on the jaw with a big sloppy kiss as Jimmy outright snapped the photo.

"Here, hold this," Jimmy casually said, putting the Uzi in Wilma's hands, which Phyllis on cue helped her hold, turning and smiling wide in the camera as Wilma happened to look down at Phyllis. That picture came out a classic, so opposite of what the image depicted. It looked like Wilma was in on this thing.

She wasn't cuffed. Wasn't crying, or looked to be in pain, or misery, or angry even. She certainly wasn't running, and even looked to be smiling, down at Phyllis while…a big laugh for them all here…sharing in holding an Uzi!

Chapter 25

"Hold up, before I take another step with ya'll, ya'll gonna half to ditch them Rumpelstiltskin rags!" Bobby said shaking his head as they started filing back into the car. "For damn sure I'm not getting on any plane with Jerry's kids," he muttered sliding back into the driver's seat about to start the car.

"That's it! That it!" Jimmy started, bouncing up and down. "Viola dressed like Cleopatra! Everyone knows Cleo was black!"

"What!?!" Bobby sat back perplexed. What was Jimmy talking about? Where did this Cleo nonsense and Viola come in?

"We've got to go in character man…" Jimmy said as if he was trying to get across a coded message. "You know," and he did the eye movement, throwing his eyes over the seat.

"All…" and Bobby dropped his shoulders and shook his head. "Man, I thought you were saying something," he huffed, reaching for the ignition again. On second thought, that dumb ass comment deserved a mush to the head, so he mushed Jimmy by the side of the head before starting the car. "You too man. You've got to come up off that hard metal rock look. Don't suit you. You too young to be looking like an aging rocker!"

"All right now, listen up everybody," Bobby said, adjusting the mirror to get a look at their faces sitting in back as he drove. "We're going to take our loot and buy us some swanky movie star fashions. And don't be long 'cause our flight leaves in an hour!"

"But—" Phyllis whimpered, about to point out how Bobby was mistaken about the time of their departure.

"—One hour," Bobby cut her off. We have to be dressed and ready!" In other words, they had to hurry, so don't quibble with him about the time.

He pulled up to a large warehouse, tucked in the furthest corner from a major intersection, just behind a large Home Depot store. Many film majors who held stage prop jobs knew all about this warehouse. It was where they shopped their clothes—from costumes to banquet attire. Reject designer clothes were shipped from all around the world here. —Thailand, China, and India mostly.

Bobby grabbed Wilma by the arm. "And old lady, don't go in here and start no funny business," he warned. "I will stick this in your behind and have you go nighty-night," he said holding up a syringe with his free hand, thumping the bottom to squirt a clear liquid.

Up to this point Wilma hadn't said too much. She seemed to be smartly going along, although looking for an opportunity to alert someone to what was going on, since Phyllis and Mona ignored her change of heart.

They entered the large tin can together, Bobby stopping them just inside the entrance. "All right now, this is the way this will work. Since you two," pointing to Mona and Phyllis, "have been playing fair, I want you," handing Mona the syringe, "to stick anyone who tries any monkey business."

Mona took the syringe and carefully stuck it in one of the many pockets hiding in the flowery pattern of her herpetologist skirt.

"Now remember, one hour! That's all we've got!"

The three of them headed to the women's section, Phyllis walking alongside Wilma, and Mona following, though somewhat giving directions.

"Right here," she said when they reached the designer suits. Mona happened to be listening to Jimmy and liked what he was saying. He was right. Wilma should be dressed liked Cleopatra, and she had a good idea what the Cleopatra in her head would look like. Easy as pie Cleopatra stood right in front of them, all of her wares hanging off a manikin.

"Phyl—I mean Tootie, take this money and buy us toiletries, and get something to decent to wear. I'll stay with her," Mona said handing her a fist full of twenties. It was crazy yeah, Mona not really understanding this part of the script, but hey, what's to reason with when you're up on stage, and on a Broadway stage at that, living your dream.

Accidentally letting down her guard, since Wilma had been playing so nicely, and since she really had no chance of escape, no matter how loud she tried to scream, she casually asked, "how do you like this get-up," admiring with her eyes the manikin she first saw.

When she heard no response from Wilma she looked over to see where her eyes were. Right on her as it turned out. She looked so hateful her skin bubbled like a boiling pot of water.

"Would you really stick me with that thing," she hissed.

"Try me," Mona hissed back, dropping the sleeve of the suit she'd been fondling to reach for the syringe.

"Excuse me Miss," Wilma abruptly spun around stopping a sales clerk passing by. "Would you mind calling the police for me? I've been kidnapped and want to report it to the police."

The sales clerk took a defensive step back from Wilma and looked instantly at Mona, startled.

"I'm sorry Miss. My mother needs to take her meds. Please don't be alarmed," Mona said, accompanied by a contrite smile. Quickly she pulled out her phone and paged Bobby, attempting to grab Wilma by the arm at the same time.

"Don't you dare touch me," Wilma shouted. "Help! Somebody please help me!"

"She's okay…it's okay…" Mona calmly said while Wilma went on shouting, though making no attempt to run. "She just needs her meds," Mona continued on, plucking the syringe as if she was preparing it by routine.

Bobby and Phyllis came running over, Bobby instantly taking hold of Wilma who then decided it was time to fight.

Double Dare

"It's okay Mom!," he said as Wilma hit him with punches so comically pathetic she might as well have been punching a pillow.

"Did you bring your mom's meds," he asked Mona, as if desperately screaming, 'stick it to her now!'

But Mona choked, and no one else but Jimmy moved, albeit to hover over Bobby vying for a good filming position. Bobby tussled with Wilma for a few seconds longer, her arms flailing like butterflies, so there really wasn't much to tussle with, another reason Mona didn't make any desperate moves, as she calmly looked around to see who was watching.

Phyllis and a few others stood off to the side, at a further distance watching. One sales clerk giggled. And a few customers muttered things. Most walked by and looked the other way, seeming quite embarrassed by Wilma's pathetic breakdown.

Please, help your mother, was the look most gave as Wilma tried to tell them what was happening.

But really? Who would believe Bobby just robbed a bank? With as calm as he and Mona ignored Wilma's tirade, rubbing her arm and patting her hand after she spent her energy during that pathetic fight, no one would believe it. A robbery like that, with bandits on the loose, would have been on the news.

One curious customer who overhead her checked the overhead TVs and saw nothing. But just to be sure, he called the police hotline and was told nothing of the sort had occurred either. On a hunch, to be even surer, he was about to question Wilma when a man wearing a silver nametag engraved: Wilcox Jeter—General Store Manager, happened by.

"Hey there Robbie, is everything okay?"

"It's my girlfriend's mother," Bobby stood up and sighed, letting Wilma's hand flop in her lap. "She's kind of schizo… or something," he said to the manager scratching his head, shamefully looking around as if he was embarrassed too.

"Geez…be careful," the manager said. He wasn't sure what was more confusing—the schizo mother or the old hippy herpetologist girlfriend.

"I hear that stuff runs in the family…" and he elbowed Bobby, as in…hint…hint…no sane man would continue on in a relationship with a woman where he learned ahead of the wedding her mother was schizo.

On that note, the customer moved on, suspicious no more, adding to the thin stream of customers who did much the same.

It was too embarrassing of a scene to believe those two nice people doing everything in their power to quiet the odd behaving woman down, not once laying a hand on her, or sticking her with that fishy needle, were trying to harm her. Kidnapping? Unlikely. Which simmered Wilma's outrageous cries down to a purr when she all on her own realized no one believed her.

At the register the sales clerk gave her a look that had her feeling an inch high tall.

"My mother has dementia," the clerk sorrowfully whispered to Mona. "I know what you must be going through," she sadly shook her head.

"Yeah, it's hard," Mona replied, piling over $1600 of merchandise on a conveyor belt, with Wilma's help, when another spastic moment hit her.

"I'll pay for my own things," Wilma lashed out. "Because I will not be participating in anything that is illegal and against the law," she shrieked like someone was pulling her hair.

But Mona turned to the clerk pensively grabbing items as if Wilma was a snapping turtle about to bite off her hand and told her to continue ringing their things. "But please hurry she added. I'm sure you know how it is..." she added. "I need to get her home and give her, her meds."

"And Mother!," she turned to hiss at Wilma. "You are scaring the clerks. I hope you don't do this on the plane, because there will be plenty of TSA agents on board who will haul you right off the plane if you act out like this!"

Chapter 26

"That was a close call," Bobby whispered to Mona as they packed the trunk with their new wares. "Do you think this will work on the plane?"

"I don't know," Mona sighed. "But she's starting to wear me down. I'm kind of regretting having taken on this project."

Silently Bobby drove to the hotel he reserved where they would change clothes before boarding a plane to Hollywood. It's where the final curtain would go up. He didn't want them dressed like starving artists for the biggest show yet to be seen, but instead like savvy business executives who knew business.

He was almost to the hotel when it hit him to ask Wilma, "say old lady, who taught you how to fight?"

All of them, including Wilma, burst out laughing, though not all at once. Jimmy, Mona, and Phyllis erupted in laughter first. Wilma's pathetic show of aggression was the funniest thing they ever saw.

She looked like a ragdoll tossing herself around. Usually when people threw one-armed punches, the other parts of their body responded in a coordinated fashion. The feet would be moving, and the face usually bearing some resemblance of a similar aggression that went with the action, but not with Wilma. Her feet remained flat on the floor while she threw lazy punches in this sort of wounding up fashion, as if she was doing a winding up exercise to throw her best shot put. That was another reason she was ignored. She fought funny.

Wilma laughed last. "Well, you just wait until I get to that airport young man. You're going to see my Kenny Norton swing!"

They were still laughing at the swinging ragdoll visual, so imagining a Kenny Norton made them laugh a little harder. "Is that the swing where you wind up both arms," Jimmy teased.

"No, it's the swing where your name better be on the bottom of your shoes," Wilma said smirking, as she gazed out the window.

And they howled more, pulling up to the hotel and spilling out of the car still howling as Bobby went through the motions passing everyone bags, peeking inside before he did.

"This one is yours…and here's yours Mo-D…and yours…" Bobby sung, until he got to Wilma's bag. He inspected the bag like the rest, handed it to her, only to be told he made a mistake.

"Why, what's wrong?" he looked at her, concerned.

"Where's my gloves?"

She may have thought she was funny, which he did oblige her with a snarly smile, but she wasn't funny in the least, and had him fooled none. It was a telling moment though; the moment where he pulled Mona aside to caution her.

"I still don't trust her," he said. "So, just stay with the skit," he warned. "Veer off the skit and we could blow it!"

All of two minutes, if that, it had taken for Bobby to deliver that message. Mona didn't even contest it, not having much to add on anyway, except for wanting to remind Bobby of all the instances he veered off script. But that would be trivial. At this moment, she was living her dream. She couldn't see it all just yet, because the footage had to be pulled off the cameras and edited, but she pined for the moment when she would see herself on screen…when she would get to critique herself, and see if she was a natural. Darn it. She just couldn't wait to see the entire thing…from start to finish—stills and all. She already imagined her and Phyllis were going to get a kick out of it, especially them stills. Magic like this just didn't happen often.

And still they had one small scene remaining…the plane ride. After that, Hollywood here they come, it would be all in the bag, which and still, they had to first get to Hollywood.

And then Bobby opened the door. About to join the others changing clothes, he opened the door to find Wilma and Phyllis rolling over the bed.

"She wanted to use the phone," Jimmy reported.

"What the—" Bobby ran over to the bed trying to separate the two. This was another oddball scrimmage. There was some grunting going on, but no words. Even Jimmy wasn't acting normal. He stood over the bed brushing his teeth and watching them wrestle.

Double Dare

Mona joined Bobby in pulling Phyllis off Wilma. What she was doing on top of Wilma was about as bizarre as Wilma doing the winding arm curls. Phyllis sort of looked like she was trying to swim across Wilma, while Wilma lying flat on her back looked like she was drowning, having fallen in a pool backwards.

"What in the hell guys?" Bobby asked, more so looking to Phyllis for an answer. "We're almost done here. Come on, don't spoil it," he practically pleaded, this being even more of his dream, another reason why Mona didn't quibble about him going off script.

"She was trying to use the phone," Phyllis panted. "I had to pin her down to stop her."

Mona might've laughed, but only if they were in Hollywood. Then none of this would've mattered, and just may have been really humorous. But they still had to get Wilma on that flight, and needed her in the right mindset. This clearly showed that she might act out, and none of them really wanted to have to sedate her.

"Look you guys," Wilma said, lifting up after Phyllis got up off the bed. "I hear judges will go a lot lighter on you if you feed your captive, and your captive says nice things about you. So, how about some room service?"

Jimmy rushed right over to Wilma, toothbrush in his mouth and paste bubbling up and frothing around his lip. "Really…you heard this," he gurgled, just before Bobby popped him in the head with a t-shirt.

"Would you go in the bathroom and finish doing that in there," Bobby fussed at him.

"But I think she's right," Phyllis said, only to quickly correct herself. "I mean the part about room service. I'm hungry."

"I think I am too," Mona agreed.

"Well, hurry up and call up for some burgers or something quick. Our flight leaves in an hour!"

"The flight still leaves in an hour," Wilma asked, cynically gazing around the room of course. "What kind of time are you guys on? That plane should've left three times by now."

"Listen old lady, we let you slide today in the store, and we're getting you something to eat, alright? So, no more wise cracks out of you or I'm going to stick you myself. You got that?"

Bobby was worried. They were closing in on the finest hour, when he could feel he was so close, yet so far away. Wilma was the hitch to a blowout ending, and he didn't want this part blown.

"Look," Wilma said looking over at Bobby sunken in a chair, "if you just clued me in to what's really going on here, maybe I can help."

Bobby stopped looking pitiful and looked over at her. "Well, you can help by getting dressed, stop trying to call the police, and stop doing those winding rounds trying to fight us!"

She still didn't look convinced, so Mona sat beside her and spoke up.

Double Dare

"I'll tell you what's going on here. You need to learn how to live lady, that's what's up. You nearly had her husband fired," she said gesturing towards Phyllis in a head nod. "That's right," she went on as Wilma's mouth fell open. "Just like you did with your husband…made him so miserable until he died of a broken heart, and now after downright killing off hordes of readers and leveling the librarian system, you are determined to continue on until you've killed off everyone's dream!"

"Wait a minute now. You don't know anything about my husband or my marriage—"

"—Yes, I do lady. That's my business. This is what I do for a living. Investigate things," Mona said, even if the market research she conducted for businesses fell along the outskirts of probing into Wilma's personal business trying to make her happy.

"All we wanted to do was fix your miserable state of mind to stop you from ruining another person's life," Mona went on. "But you are proving to be impossible to fix."

"You mean to tell me you think that by kidnapping me, and taking my personal things is the way to make me cheer up," Wilma asked looking from Bobby to Mona. Phyllis had gone into bathroom to get dressed. Jimmy was standing by the door looking in a mirror, humming and straightening his necktie as if no one was talking in the room.

"Yes, we actually did," Mona said, meaning every word. "This young man sitting beside me has a dream to have his script—"

"—ssst!" Bobby looked up alarmed. The spiel was so moving he thought he was listening to one of the Dooby Brothers, until she decided to tie on that little twist at the end. She was worse than some actors who tried to jazz up a script by throwing in their own little musty lines without understanding the storyline.

"Lady, would you please just do us all a big favor and dress in the clothes we bought you. We're not killers, or bank robbers, or anything else. We just want you to have fun and enjoy the time we're taking to spend with you."

"Yeah," Jimmy called from the mirror. "So act nice or we're suing you to get all our money back if we don't win this film fest!"

Chapter 27

All was honky dory when they checked out of the hotel. There were a few jokes exchanged at the counter when the front desk clerk asked how was their stay and Jimmy chimed, "in and out at $189…how do you think our stay was?"

The clerk didn't ask any more questions after that, and they all rolled out of there laughing…Wilma too, looking very much like the chocolate-skinned Egyptian Cleopatra, after letting Mona wrap up that forehead to round off those corners. Between that, the inch-long lashes and new drawn on eyes, she was a new woman.

The drive to the airport was about the same, Jimmy keeping the humor going, and Wilma seeming to play along. Phyllis and Mona even got in a call to Joe and Frank to let them know they were about to fly out, and that everything was all honky dory.

"Joe is going to be floored when he hears what all happened," Phyllis chuckled, tickled about Joe telling her how relieved he was that he didn't have to deal with Wilma that day.

"Yeah, well wait until you have to explain how many of those cameras we sold, " Mona reminded her.

"Oh yeah," Phyllis sighed. She forgot about that part, but by her expression quickly remembered.

"But don't worry Phyl—we'll think of something," Mona said patting her leg. "I just thank you so much for going along with all of this…making my dream so real. This will last between us forever."

"Yeah, but what about her?" Phyllis nodded off to where Wilma sat—sort of off to herself, meaning she chose not to sit near any of them.

"What do you think'll make her happy? Or at least act like she's having fun?"

Mona watched Wilma for a minute, reading glasses hanging off the bridge of her nose, leg crossed at the ankle, holding a newspaper up in the air in front of her face, as two small children ran in circles nearby. "I bet that woman is having more fun right now, than she's ever had in her life," Mona concluded.

"Really," Phyllis asked, not seeing the same thing.

"Welp, time will tell," Mona added as Jimmy came animatedly bouncing over to report what they, and everyone sitting in the area heard over the PA system.

"—Hey you two, they're about to board," he said, giving them the googly ut-oh…it's time eyes.

Each of them knew real law enforcement would be on the flight, not that Wilma couldn't have crushed the film during the security screening. But here's where she could really crush, not only their dream, but their spirits. Eventually, and perhaps, they might be cleared of all wrongdoing, but it would come at the expense of missing out on entering the contest. And entering next year wasn't any good either. The stakes were high, a lot had been invested. It just had to work.

"Is it me, or are they making these seats smaller," Phyllis, taking the window seat, said when a woman a row ahead of them turned to sssh them.

"I'm sorry," the woman lifted up to apologize over the seat. "It's just that I just got my baby to sleep and you all are being a little loud."

The three of them sitting together looked at each other after the woman turned around. The last thing either of them wanted to hear was a fussy baby for five hours in this tight boxed in space. But it was something about the way the woman asked them to 'keep it down' that rubbed all three of them wrong.

"Wait Wilma, no," Mona said tugging the hem of her jacket. "New mother's think the world revolves around them and their sleeping brats."

Wilma slid back down in her seat. "I was just going to offer earplugs for the child," Wilma chuckled.

"They make earplugs for babies," Phyllis squealed across Wilma to Mona.

"Yes—"

"—Honestly, this is really rude you know," the woman said, popping up over the seat again. "I just asked if you could hold it down. There's no need for you to behave like this."

"Why do we have to be miserable just because you're on this flight?" Mona argued back. "And you're talking louder than any of us!"

Just so happened, a flight attendant was passing by. Promptly the woman tugged her sleeve, making the attendant lean over to hear her gripe. They exchanged words; nothing they in the row behind could make out. When the mumbling stopped, the flight attendant lifted up and asked if they could please hold it down.

"Yeah Mo—" Jimmy said sitting in the row of seats in the opposite aisle (since given up using codes names), "if you wouldn't mind holding down some of that breathing too. In fact—"

—and Phyllis squealed…loud enough to make the flight attendant turn around and issue another stern warning. "I'll have Marshalls remove you from this flight if this continues," she said, panning a mean glare across the row at the five of them, plus an innocent traveler sitting between Jimmy and Bobby.

"I'm sorry, please accept our apologies," Mona said. "We're just trying to get comfortable, but promise not to talk for the rest of the trip." She rolled her eyes when the flight attendant moved on. "Some nerve," she hissed at Wilma seated in the middle. "I still remember when flying used to be a Class-A way to travel, but not anymore. Pretty soon Greyhound will have these air crooks beat."

Ms. Pretty Fed Up in the row ahead sighed noisily, which prompted Wilma to thump the back of the seat with her knee. The woman didn't jump up that time, but only because the plane started climbing in the air. Through the seats they watched her knuckles turn pale gripping the arm as the plane did its climb. But once the plane reached cruising altitude, they continued their conversation.

Double Dare

Wilma turned the lever to the tray in front of her and let it drop down. "Oh, that's right. Forgot about the cutbacks," she pouted. "Five hour flights don't serve meals anymore."

"You think we're allowed—"

—and they looked over to see Phyllis pulling on the seat to rise. "Excuse me," she said in her normal high-pitched sharp ragged tone. "I need to use it…" she chuckled.

The woman didn't make a move through any of this either, even if they could feel her fury and almost see a smokestack rising above the bale of frazzled dry hair clumped on her head.

"You know Wilma," and Mona was sure she used her inside voice turned down to its lowest notch because she didn't want Jimmy and Bobby sitting on the other side of the aisle to hear her. "I really appreciate you going along with us on this project. At first I was starting to think I bit off more than I could chew."

Wilma smiled warmly, a face Mona didn't think the woman could make. She hardly recognized the warden in her, which too may have had something to do with the Cleopatra look she wore so well.

"But now, I have one question to ask you," Wilma whispered using her inside voice turned down as well. "Tell me exactly what kind of project is this?"

"We're helping Bobby make a film," she whispered. "Only this one isn't like the typical 72-hour film projects.

This is a 120-hour deal," and she couldn't help but squeal laughing, out loud.

That did it. The woman was up again, jumping up a whole foot over the seat, a fraction of a second after the baby started squealing.

"You two are impossible!" the woman spat, eyes looking on them with the pity of a honey badger. "You two are the most despicable animals I have ever flown with in my entire life!" she spewed, teeth resembling sawed off pinking shears.

"Yeah lady, and you must've mated with one of my relatives because that ain't no angel you got on your hands either," Wilma laughed.

"Mo—Chihuahuas don't exactly count as vermin," Jimmy said, adding in his two bits just as the same flight attendant rushed to the scene.

"I demand another seat," the woman cried a hair lower than her baby.

"Oh, gee-whiz…come on, this really sucks!" moaned a passenger in the row behind them.

This was the moment Wilma used to excuse herself to use the restroom, passing Phyllis in aisle as she was returning to her seat. Other passengers had joined the crusade, so chaos and confusion abound, since Mona and Jimmy weren't finished heaving salt on this open wound.

"Come on guys," Bobby pleaded, seeing the flight attendant storming the aisle headed straight for them, looking finished with negotiating on that flight. "We're almost there. Don't ruin things now!"

But it was too late. A TSA agent and that Marshall the flight attendant warned she'd sic on them stepped forward, flipping out badges and commandeering the row they sat on to chaperone them for the reminder of the flight to Hollywood.

Chapter 28

While the woman sat comfortably in first class with her bawling baby, TSA Agent Phil Jawoski sat between Jimmy and Bobby, and Deputy Marshall Lemmons sat between Mona and Phyllis. Both men, a hair shorter than Mount Everest, and a few pounds lighter than one adult elephant, forbade them to speak when Mona only wanted to ask, "Where was Wilma?"

Wilma never returned to her seat. She slipped away during the commotion and they hadn't seen hide nor hair of her since. The plane landed and still no Wilma. Mona saw Jimmy once try to turn around, seeming to have the same question she did, but when big Jaw jabbed him in the gut, Mona took that as her warning to keep quiet until it was time to speak.

They were escorted off the plane first, Bobby muttering this was not a part of the script. Jaw led and Lame Lemmons held up the rear. Silently and single file they were led to that one famed room. The hanging room. The one with five or six chairs, a table, and a bright white light hanging above.

"All right, which one of you masterminded that foiled hostage attempt?" Jaw bellowed.

The four of them slowly turned to look at each other. What? What in the hell was this Nick Nolte impersonator talking about? They weren't even close to terrorists. They were a body of artists, students, and housewives for heavens sake.

Double Dare

"We didn't—"

"—Shut up! Was I speaking to you?" Jaw shouted in Jimmy's face, spit flying in all directions.

Jimmy leaned over, throwing up an elbow trying to ward off his voice as much as the spit, earning him another jab in the gut; this time in the side.

"Are you trying to fight me?" Jaw leaned over more, shouting in Jimmy's face. "Move again nurf boy and I'll charge you with assault with a puny weapon! Boy…" he growled, "I could get you for ten to life!"

Obviously this had to be a crude joke, although as unreal as it all seemed, the threat remained. No one cared to jump up to test how authentic this type of interrogation might be.

"Bill," Jaw said to Lame Lemmons, "I think we need to split these parasites up! Get Gracy and Zelda in here to deal with these two. We'll take the wimps!"

Phyllis looked over at Jimmy and Bobby, pleading that they tell her by a motion of the eyes if this perhaps was a part of the script.

"Are you two exchanging more signals?" Jaw bent down to yell in Jimmy's face. "Hurry up Bill," he said rising up, away from the shrinking fast Jimmy. "Hurry up and get these parasites split up before we have to call in street-moppers to mop up this mess!"

Minutes later Bill brought back Gracy and Zelda, looking like Jaw's and Bill's mother and grandmother. Zelda was taller than Jaw and Bill, combined. And her voice was heavier than both men's combined too. She also had more facial hair, and her hands didn't look like they belonged to her. Her hands in fact, didn't look like they belonged to any human. Mona could have sworn she only saw three fingers when she grabbed her by the arm leading her to a smaller room. The first thing she thought was an ostrich was on the loose.

"Young lady, you are in a heap of trouble. We might have to draft an order to have you extradited back to Colombia," Zelda said, throwing one foot up on the chair beside her.

Mona looked down at Zelda's foot, too. It had to be a size 24-shoe she slapped down on that chair. Her foot was so big it stopped her from thinking about how much trouble they might be in because she could only think about feet. Who made shoes for feet that big? And was that a shoe on her foot? Actually, was that even a foot?

But Colombia? Did Zelda mean Columbia as in one of the Columbia's in the states somewhere? Columbia, Maryland maybe? Because if she did, she was mistaken there too. She hadn't been to Columbia, Maryland since 9th grade on a field trip.

"We'll let those Mexicalies deal with you!" Zelda grinned, evilly of course.

Good one! What a great line, for whoever slipped it in the script. And Zelda wasn't all that bad of an actor, either. She really knew how to juice up Mexico, using her couchy-grouchy wicked tone to make the place sound wickeder.

"But…but…I've never even been to Mexico," Mona protested, her first words since being so wrongly and unlawfully detained.

"Good! That'll teach you smart wannabes about breaking the law!" Zelda retorted.

"But breaking which law? We didn't do anything," Mona pleaded.

"Yeah…yeah…that's what they all say!"

It was a little difficult to tell what was going on, but watching Zelda swaying her exaggerated behind much too gaudy to be real, as she left out of the mock interrogation room, she had to assume they were still within the vicinity of a script. She just wasn't sure whose script. Poor Bobby kept saying it wasn't his, but it had to be someone's. Maybe he was getting help?

Chapter 29

Zelda left her sitting in a room where a wise joker must have thought she would talk if they turned up the air. Zelda also left behind a pack of cheese crackers, likely made with the batch that was packaged when saran wrapped foods first came out, probably thinking hunger pains might speed up her wanting to talk too. The thing was, Mona had seen all these tricks played out on screen, many times over. Besides, she had a nice big fat deluxe cheeseburger at the hotel, thanks to Wilma's insistence. And too, what did they want her to talk about. Like, what was the question?

She tried calling Frank, after twenty minutes of debating if she should, but found she had no service. So she was stuck with guessing whether there was still a script left she could break.

"Chow time," Zelda bellowed as she opened the door using one large padlock key. "Maybe some good hot food will get you terrorists to talking."

Zelda led her to a large cafeteria where she met up with the others. Their coloring went from silvery-white, to pinkish-green. Bobby fell in the middle, a sea-crest blue.

"Did anyone get their one phone call?" Mona asked soon as she noticed they were free from the Jaw-spitting three-fingered wardens.

"Call who to say what," Jimmy scoffed as Bobby charged at her. "Why did do that," Bobby cried. "That wasn't in the script! You ruined this!"

Double Dare

Mona threw out her arms. "Bobby, I'm—"

"—Move it! Move it, boys and girls! You've got 10-minutes to pick, choose, and eat!"

It was another warden ordering them around, this one a lot nicer looking, though wielding a club she batted against her palm.

"Come on you guys…this has to be a joke," Mona said. "I say we stick this out just a little bit longer."

"Yeah, Bobby," Jimmy mocked. "Let's wait until they walk us out on the yard and line us up against that brick wall and pull the safeties off their mallets!"

"Mo," Phyllis whimpered, chiming in off to her left, "I think we need to put an end to this and ask to call an attorney."

"Please Phyl—have any of you not been listening to these extraditing fools. Do you really think they're actually going to let you call someone to stop this unlawful detaining?"

"But where's Wilma? Phyllis asked.

Mona looked at Bobby. It was the grand seventy-five thousand question.

"I think Mo is right," Bobby finally agreed. "We have to push on. Besides, it's not like we really have much of a choice at this point."

"Ooo!" Jimmy started dancing, turning around to show off a lobster tail he picked up off the buffet. "I think I want to stay. I don't want to go back. It's settled. This is my home," and he kissed the tail, before closing his eyes to dramatize his palate romancing the flavors roaming over his tongue.

The three of them scurried up to the buffet with that sighting. A seafood feast out of the deepest bluest waters stretched 30-feet or more before their eyes.

"Did she say 10-minutes?"

"Time's up," the baton-batting warden bellowed, standing in the doorway.

But Jimmy ignored the warden. He had already lost his mind, stuffing his Oscar dela-Rente suit with as many lobster tails as he could fit in each pocket.

"Boy, where do you think you're going with that," the baton batting warden stopped Jimmy. "Do you realize you are about to enter a court of law!"

The three of them—Bobby, Phyllis, and Mona, each taking a bite out of a sea creature stopped in the midst of this bite to look at each other. About to enter court?

"Wait! Hold it!" Bobby stepped up to the miss-cast baton-batting warden. "We know our rights lady. We demand to speak to an attorney. And we demand our one phone call," he said, as he went on to finish off his sea creature, chewing wildly.

"Boy, who you gettin' smart with," and the miss-cast baton-wielding warden turned away, yelling for Jaw. "Jawoski!" she yelled down the hallway, causing Mona to dump the contents in her mouth in a napkin at the sound of hearing that man's name.

"Jawoski! This boy says he knows his rights! He wants one of them fancy high-priced lawyers, and to call his mama!"

Jawoski showed up, with Zelda and her daughter breathing over his shoulder like two thirsty dragons.

"Who wants an attorney? Which one of these pesticides said they want to call their mommy?"

"That one—"

"—I said it," Bobby stepped forward, moving aside the baton the warden held against his chest. "I know my rights, and demand to speak with an attorney. On the double!"

"Awl sooky-sooky," Gracy laughed. "The boy's got balls…"

"Listen here, boy with balls," Jaw leered at Bobby, speaking nose to nose. "You're about to get your due process smarty pants. And in case you don't know what that is, which I assume you do not since you're in here squealing like an eel after we fed you numskulls like kings and queens. That means you're about to get a speedy trial."

Jaw moved away from Bobby to address them all. "Ya'll just don't know how good ya'll brats have it. You're about to make living history here…" and he laughed crudely. "You'll be the very first in history to have speediest trial ever!"

"But we haven't even made our plea—"

"—Plea? What we need with your plea boy? We know the law. Ya'll don't. We'll figure out whether you're guilty or not!"

Chapter 30

"Here Ye'! Here Ya'll! Ya'all rise!" bellowed a bailiff who had to stand on a desk to be seen. He also had to speak in a microphone that made his voice stretch out, otherwise he would've sounded really squeaky, and for those in the back, they wouldn't have known he was even in the courtroom.

"Oh, what's next," Jimmy leaned in to whisper to Bobby as they sat back down. "King Arthur and—"

—Whack! Jaw hit Jimmy from behind, upside the head. "Look, listen, and learn something boy!"

"Ouch," Jimmy whined rubbing his neck. "Do you think we can get this guy to cut back on some of the abuse," he whispered to Bobby again.

Whack! Jaw smacked him again, bringing Jimmy off the bench and spinning around this time.

"Listen here buddy. I've about had it up to—"

"—come on Jimmy man," Bobby said tugging on his sleeve as Jaw stood, towering over him. "Cool it." And he had to whisper this part himself too. "I think I found us a way out of here."

That put Jimmy on ice, but only for a second. Judge Arthur, costumed dramatically like King Arthur in an assortment reference books, appeared from behind a hidden door and moved to the throne.

"All for Christ's sake, you've got to be kidding me! That's awful!" Jimmy moaned loudly. Jaw didn't swat him that time, but only because he started laughing, along with everyone else—the bailiff who hopped off the table, spectators, Gracy and Zelda, Mona, Bobby, Phyllis...everyone in the courtroom. Phyllis laughed the loudest, and hardest.

"Oh God...oh God..." Phyllis panted, wheezing and failing her arms for air. "This is hilarious," she laughed to tears.

"He looks like fucking Peter Pan," Jimmy said. "Who dressed that guy? The costume designer needs to be fired, then spanked, squashed, and sued."

To be fair, Judge Arthur held a blade and wore a crown. He also wore body armor—that medieval stuff middle-age knights wore. His armor though was a mesh of recycled materials dyed green, nothing that would withstand a halfway decent fencing match. That mesh bodysuit would come apart like a loosely knotted crochet sweater, right along with the green chinchilla mink and that goofy smile smeared across his face. Didn't he know people didn't smile back then? But then too, who wouldn't smile if they had to walk in a courtroom, in the present day, wearing green leotards and shoes that curled way up at the toe.

"Another outburst from you young man and you'll be held in contempt of court," said Judge Arthur.

"Oh Judge Pan, I'm deeply sorry and very scared," Jimmy jeered. "Please don't wave your magic sword at me. You might turn me into Harry Potter..." Jimmy chuckled like Saint Nick, although instead of ho, ho, ho...he used "Ha! Ha! Ha!"

Judge Arthur rolled his eyes, largely deciding to ignore Jimmy, and instead bellowed, "Ugh Counsel... how does your client plead!?!"

"Hey Peter," Jimmy called out again. "Who are you talking to buddy? There's no counsel at this table. Only felons. All convicts who decided to dress up for you today," and he held up his wrists and shook them. "See...no arm bracelets," he smiled. "Only suits!"

"Who's responsible for these people," Judge Arthur roared, this time coming out with his tough voice, losing the smile and some of his patience.

Jimmy looked around, smugly smiling, as Bobby, Phyllis, and Mona stared in open amused delight. No one said a word.

"You mean to tell me these people have no legal counsel?"

And still nothing.

"Ugh, Mabel," Judge Arthur said to some random spectator sitting among the audience. "Go sit at that table and try to represent that clown and his pals."

"All...this is so bad it's pathetic," Jimmy groaned shaking his head.

"Hey," and he stood to address the courtroom. "Whoever producing this one, I would say kill it while you still have some of your budget left, except since it's obvious to see King Arthur's costume has already taken care of that part, I say kill it while you still have some dignity left."

Meanwhile, Mabel scurried over to the table, to whisper in Jimmy's ear. "Come on, stop it please. Marty really worked hard to put this together. Be fair."

Jimmy turned right to Bobby. "Up! Told you. It's a wrap, Marty steals the day!"

"Remove that fella from this court," yelled Judge Arthur. "Get him out of here, now!"

Panicked, hearing Jimmy's comment and knowing right away what kind of trouble they were in, Mona looked over at Bobby as two extras rushed over to the table and muscled Jimmy out of the courtroom.

"Stay with the script," she muttered, kicking Bobby in the shin. But he seemed to ignore her, so she kicked him harder. "Stay with—"

"—It's your fault—"

"—the defense wishes to plea," Mabel announced, distracting Bobby and Mona from divvying the blame.

"Great," stated Judge Arthur, "but since they can't possibly be pleading to everything, the prosecutors are going to start calling their witnesses."

Chapter 31

Jawoski let them keep their hotel reservations, since formal charges hadn't yet been filed. But if they tried to avoid the mock trial, and leave California, they could do so at the risk of officially becoming real wanted fugitives; the kind posted in the post office. Their next trial, he promised, would be anything but a mock.

Mona didn't want to upset Bobby but... "I can't believe this! They're stealing our script!" she fumed, pacing in front of a window, so ironically facing an icon that thrilled her to finally see—the Hollywood sign.

She looked over at him, lying back on the bed and staring up at the ceiling like a dead man in a wide flowery casket.

"I can't believe someone would do this," she said again. "I mean, this isn't even a case of stealing a quote or a phrase, or even a whole idea, but this creep, whoever he is, is blatantly stealing all of our footage!"

"I can," Jimmy said. "I know him. Marty is a creep. He was in a Chem class with me once. Pissed in a bottle and tried to pass it off as some kind of discovery to saving gas. But that piece of shit was exposed before his piss even made it to the lab. The instructor read his notes. Dumb ass genius copied them straight from the damn textbook."

"Geez," Mona sighed, looking over at Phyllis already dressed for bed—Bugs Bunny fluffy slippers, flannel pajama set with blue piping running around the collar, and large sponge rollers tucked beneath a fluffy nightcap. "I made dinner reservations tonight, hoping to celebrate our first night here…but—"

"—but let's hold off on that and save it for our last meal," Jimmy wryly added. "I'm not much up for eating, not unless we're talking about roasting Peter Pan."

"My granddaddy always said, 'if you lie, you'll cheat, and if you cheat you'll steal'," Phyllis yawned, shaking her head as she calmly unpacked her suitcase. "Here," she said pulling a Bible from a drawer she was putting her clothes in. "Bet my grandfather read that quote somewhere in here."

Jimmy and Mona looked at each other. On the opposite end of Bobby's despair had to be Phyllis's oblivion. Note to self: Clearly at this point they were the only hope to figuring this thing out.

"It's like this," Jimmy continued on, "Marty has no morals or ethics. He failed those classes too. He's hopeless. He's never going to amount to anything. So I say we put him out of his misery."

"Wait Jimmy," Mona said holding up her hand to Phyllis's loud hums, making it clear who she was leaning on in their great time of need. "We already have a kidnapping charge hanging over us. We don't want them to throw the book at us and kick away the stool too!"

"Yeah, I guess I see your point. But—"

"—but there has to be a way to stop this Marty person. Which by the way," and Mona looked around the room, making sure the comatose Bobby and humming

Phyllis knew she was addressing them too. "Has anyone seen Wilma?"

"Find Marty and you'll find Wilma," Jimmy hissed. "I wouldn't be surprised if they—hey—I have an idea!" he said, his face lightening up as a brilliant idea tackled him mid-thought.

"That woman is almost near a hundred, right?"

"Jimmy no, she's not," Mona smirked, trying not to laugh too. "She probably has 30 more years to go. You'll be closer to 100 before she'll be a 100."

"Darn! I was going to say we could claim she was senile. You know, like if we had to go to a real trial."

Mona chuckled and slumped down on the loveseat. "I think we need to sleep on this one…attack it from fresh new minds in the morning."

Chapter 32

Judge Arthur let Jimmy back in the mock courtroom, this being after dragging Phyllis to the courthouse when she awoke to a new stream of consciousness that wanted to call Joe and give him a newer update on what was happening.

"I promise Phyl—after today we'll call the guys and tell them what's happening," Mona bribed her, hoping, like Jimmy that they might find that needle in the haystack to get the film back on track.

"But there might not be another day. They could haul us in today and that would be it!" Phyllis cried.

"Honestly Phyl—" Jimmy interjected. "We would've been in jail…probably beneath it, if they really had something to go on."

It was an offhand remark, but one of those 'oh so right' remarks. Mona could feel it. They were getting warm, even if Bobby by this point had turned into somewhat of a robot. The part they were missing was right in the middle of this anemic remark.

Judge Arthur looked worse than the day before. Still had the same big goofy-looking eyes, but he traded the Peter Pan costume in for a floor-length blue velour robe he wore over a powder blue all-in-one body suit. He looked like he could fly—in the sky without a chute.

"Why not just draw an 'S' on his chest," Jimmy snickered, only for Mona to hear however.

"What? That green wasn't working for you judge," he laughed for the court and the judge to hear.

Judge Arthur only rolled his eyes and looked over at the opposite table.

"Prosecution, please call your witness."

There was a crowd at the prosecution's table, to their measly one Mabel who hadn't said two words to them since being assigned the role. But dressed in day-old suits, pearls, and neckties, like a hornet of wasps the group huddled at the prosecution table nudged and poked each other eager to introduce the first witness. "Let me…let me…" they buzzed.

"Which one is Marty," Mona whispered in Jimmy's ear. She just wanted to see what he looked like, imagining a short tubby kid no one would have noticed had he not been directing and producing the film.

"You won't see him 'til the end. He's a coward too," Jimmy said as a door behind them clapped closed.

Everyone turned to see who was walking in, to include Mona, and Jimmy who stood the moment he recognized it was Wilcox!

Extending his arms in disbelief, and mouth hanging open, Jimmy jeered, "awl Will…how you gonna do me like this? I thought we was like this," and he tapped his chest with two fingers, a known gang gesture, which the grand treat in appreciating this gesture was taking in how Jimmy dressed for this performance.

Three quarter high-top black All-star Converse sneakers—tied tight and double-knotted. Nantucket plaid pants—long and fitted, though not long enough to hide the orange socks. He also wore a blazer, a beige pinstripe blazer—possibly one his mother dressed him in for Easter, when he was two. It was tight and wouldn't button. The sleeves barely met his elbow, and they weren't rolled up. The hem of the blazer rested just above his navel, which was exposed due to the fact he wore a t-shirt he decided to tie into a knot around his waist. But being a skinny kid this get-up worked for him. He didn't look nearly as bad as the judge in the strange powder blue body suit.

Mona tapped his arm. "Jimmy stop it, before the judge throws you out again," she said just as the judge warned it was exactly what would happen if he made another outburst.

Wilcox pledged to tell the whole truth, and nothing but the whole truth, but began his testimony lying through his teeth.

"—and so, it was then when I turned," which Wilcox melodramatically twisted his body to show the court. "Hearing this pitiful woman's cries, all I saw was this skinny kid who I'd seen in the store many times, standing over her, and pounding her...oh dear Lord it was so horrible," Wilcox cried, bringing his hands to his face and yucking so hard his shoulders vibrated.

"Oh, for crying out loud!" Jimmy moaned loudly, throwing up his hands. "I can't believe that sissy!"

Double Dare

Judge Arthur banged the gavel on his desk as the courtroom filled with sounds of outrage; moaning and sobbing, and shifting uncomfortably in their seats.

"I'm warning you! One more outburst and you're out of here!"

Wilcox continued, following the prosecutor's next instruction, which was to point out the culprit he saw beating the helpless old woman like a dirty straw mat.

Proud and sure of himself Wilcox stood tall, poked out his round chest, and said in a loud clear voice, "Your honor, it was him. I'd know that face anywhere. He did it. Jimmy Jackson Jeeps!" he said pointing a quivering finger directly at Jimmy.

"Awl fuck you! Blow it out your asshole, Uncle dick. You fuckin' suck!"

"Quiet! Quiet! Quiet in the court!" Judge Arthur cried, viscously beating the gavel against the desk.

"Now, you young man," Judge Arthur said, lazily pointing the gavel at Jimmy. "I think I've already warned you enough times—"

—but the judge's admonishing was interrupted by someone in the back sending him a signal. Mona couldn't see who was in the back of the courtroom sending the signals, but she saw the judge looking back that way before interrupting himself.

"You may step down sir," he sympathetically said to Wilcox before turning to face the prosecutor. "Will you please call your next witness."

"You blow man," Jimmy hissed at Wilcox as he walked by the defense table. He also took the gum he'd been chewing and threw it at Wilcox, hitting him in the forehead. It stuck, right there square in the center.

They looked up to next see one of the clerk's that had been in the store that day taking the stand. She already had her hand raised, swearing to tell the whole truth, and nothing but the whole truth, but like Wilcox, they could already see she was about to lie through her teeth just by the way she was dressed.

"Hey Lucretia babycakes," Jimmy mocked. "Amish women don't carry condoms in their bonnets darling."

"I've had about enough of you young man," Judge Arthur said, interrupting the woman's testimony.

But "yah, yah, yah," Jimmy dryly laughed, wiped out from a near full day's worth of blatant lying. "You said that already. You've been saying that since we got here! Why don't you try acting on it, Judge Smurfy."

Chapter 33

Each of them chose to dine forty feet closer to heaven for varied reasons; to get a closer look at the stars...to isolate themselves from the looming obvious...to look at the problem once more from afar...to be among like company. To simply say they'd been somewhere they hadn't been before. All those reasons were up there, plus one more.

"Jimmy, really" Phyllis sighed heavily, "you should stop with the outbursts. You're making the judge mad."

"Well, he's making me mad too, which I hope you realize, he's no real judge," Jimmy said turning a bottle of beer up to his mouth. "Aaah!" he smacked. "For some reason, I feel good tonight!"

Bobby, sitting across from Jimmy, wanted to smile wider than he was, taking in his infectious character, but he was still a little wiped out about his pet project being swiped from beneath his feet the way it was. "I'm glad one of us is having fun," he said.

"We have to stop them. We just have to," Mona muttered. It was no way she could let someone get away so blatantly with stealing their project like that.

"Well, I'm calling Joe!" Phyllis said, grabbing her purse from beneath the table about to rise from her seat.

"Phyl—please..." Mona pleaded, casting a discreet look in Bobby's direction. "I didn't come all this way for nothing. Besides, Joe is going to be looking for results. I don't think either of them would have been all chirpy about this trip if they thought we were going to be out here blowing more money on having fun."

Slowly Phyllis plopped back down in the seat. "Oh yeah, I keep forgetting about that. The last three times I talked to him, he kept asking how many buyers had we found," she ruefully chuckled.

"I just hope you guys know I really appreciate you sticking out your neck and hanging in here with me on this," Bobby offered in the bummed out voice. "But it's always next year," he shrugged. "Who knows... I might win a lottery and get another shot at financing another one of these."

"All, now that sounded pretty pathetic," Jimmy laughed. He pushed the beer bottle into Bobby's chest and playfully teased, "man, where's that fighting spirit! I would've never agreed to do this if I didn't think your idea was off the chizz-ain!" And he leaned back in his chair to toast to the sky, nearly falling over backwards.

"Ooo! Watch it Jimmy!" Mona jumped, reaching for the chair.

"Man, I think you better hold up on those brews... and do like Phyl is saying...stop irritating the dude. I think—"

Jimmy hopped up. "—I think I've got it! Yes! I think I finally do have it!"

The three of them looked up, studying him closely, watchful, and waiting, and really hopeful.

There was no denying, parodying this skit had its dark moments, but overall the skit was like nothing they could've ever dreamed being involved in, and they had a lot of fun making it happen. They wanted this to work. It had to work. Though most of all, none of them could stomach seeing the project totally swiped out of their hands. They'd rather come in last place, than be defeated this way. If Marty won off their hard work, they would have to tie up his winnings in real court.

"You see how you keep saying I should tone it down," Jimmy started in this dim cagey voice. "…And how the Judge is going to throw me out of court if I keep it up. Well, why is it that he didn't do it today. He kept threatening to do it, but notice how he never once followed through on the threats?"

They had. Mona even recalled someone from the back of the court so obviously gesturing for the judge to ignore Jimmy. But why was that?

"I'll tell you why," Jimmy went on. "He needs me there. I'm the only one in that courtroom making his stinkin' stolen film work!"

"Ah Jimmy," Phyllis chimed in. "Then wouldn't this be more of a reason to pipe down?"

"No, it wouldn't," Jimmy answered, showing on his face he really might have it. "Because the more I keep clowning, the more comfortable they will become—"

"—O-O-O! I got it too!" Mona cheered excitedly. She wasn't exactly on the same page as Jimmy, but pretty close she imagined.

"Can't you guys see? We've got something they do not," Mona stared wild eye at a hopeful and surprised Bobby and Phyllis. "We've got the original script," she said bugling her eyes. "They don't have that footage which…ahem…happens to be the damning testimony that will blow their little case sky high out of the water, while—"

"—aah," Jimmy sighed, eyes twinkling. "Let this be your lesson kids, when at first you learn to deceive."

Mona looked over at Bobby and saw his peewee chest rising and collapsing, hoping defeat was about to move inside. Please tell him they were on to something, his little heaving chest timidly spoke. He had forgotten the early footage, not that any of them knew exactly where Mona was leading them, but they were sure she was on to something with her eyes round as the moon.

"But we only have two days left. How—"

"—We're going to follow the script is how," Mona concluded.

"But what if they push this all the way to the deadline, which I feel is what they're already doing," Bobby said, having thought through this angle, trying to salvage what he could. If they hold the trial until the tail end, then there'd be no time to edit.

"No Bobby. They have the same amount of time as we do in the editing room. The only difference is, we have the original script, something they've taken for granted." She looked at both Phyllis and Jimmy for her next pitch. "This is why we must stick to the script, and keep to our same courtroom behavior, amped up or down, depending on what's happening."

Bobby smiled wide. "Gosh, I hope this works."

"It will work. And damn it, we're going to have us some fun while we make it work!"

"But what about Wilma?"

"Wilma's swimming wif de fishes," Jimmy teased, holding his fork between his upper lip and nose.

"All right now," Mona warned. "Don't over do it Jimmy. This all could still backfire on us."

Chapter 34

"—Wait a minute now Phyl—we just talked the other night," Joe cried in the phone. "You told me you and Mo were selling like crazy and out having a chunky good time...standing in a few of the stars shoes. But who's shoes were they Phyl? —Snipes?"

Phyllis pulled the phone away from her ear and down below her chest, to give Mona who stood there watching the 'what do I say now,' look?

"Tell him we need them to come out here, to help us work the cameras," Mona mostly whispered, partly mouthed. After their discovery Bobby and Jimmy had gathered a few of the cameras, trying to see what they could pull off them. But not being experts with the device, they had a few questions; questions Phyllis bungled asking after greeting Joe with the troubling voice.

"Here...give me the phone," Mona sighed, taking the phone out of Phyllis's hand.

"Hey Joe!" she said all upbeat. "Mo—here. What Phyl is trying to ask is, how do we work these cameras if we wanted to put the footage in another type of format?"

Joe hesitated. He wasn't a slow man. Something was going on, and before he answered, he wanted to get to the bottom of it.

"Phyl said ya'll are in a bind. What's going on out there Mo—"

"Awl Joe, you know how Phyl is. She sees all these big time movie producers and is scared we won't be able to show them what we have," tossing in, "can't make no loot, with no boot."

They told Joe and Frank most of the truth about what they were doing, only leaving out the one small clip—the clip about kidnapping Wilma. But Joe needed no more coaxing. He knew how to work the cameras, and always wanted to see Hollywood. He packed as Mona sugarcoated.

"Now, let me call Frank," Mona said after speaking with Joe. "Now that you've opened a whole new can of worms, I'll have to tell him the truth," she got out before Frank answered her call.

"Hey sweetheart, how are things?"

"You tell me Mo? Ya'll are the ones out there in Hollywood."

"Oh well, we've pretty much wrapped up the hardest part of shooting the movie. Now we're trying to edit this thing," she said trying to put a smile in her voice, looking at Phyllis standing next to her watching with the rigid eagle eyes.

"That's great. Now ya'll will be back in a day or two, right?"

"Yep," she edged out. "In a day or two," she cringed.

"Yeah, Joe has been by here a couple of times, talking about all the big wheelers Phyllis has been dealing with," Frank said in his bothered voice. "He's running around here telling everyone ya'll are out there setting Hollywood on fire."

Oh God, Mona muttered beneath her breath, letting her head drop…when it hit her!

"Hey hun," she said jerking her head up. "Don't let this freak you out when I tell you this. Phyl didn't want to tell Joe that we could go to prison for a long time if we don't get these cameras working right."

"Huh!?!" Frank uttered noisily, switching the phone to the other ear in case the other one wasn't working right. And double a 'huh' for Phyllis's eyes jumping out of its sockets.

She ignored them, drawing out a convoluted tale about a producer who felt wronged by Phyllis trying to pawn off the cameras. He had them going through a mock trial, she explained, to help decide whether he wanted to press official charges and turn them over to face a real jury of few peers. In part it was sort of true. Just switch out the cameras for kidnapping Wilma.

"So hun," she went on, "Please don't let Joe know any of this. Just try to do what you can to convince him how important it is that we get these cameras to work."

Mona could hear Phyllis silently cheering behind her. 'Yes! Yes! That's it! Good one Mo—' she chanted. Why hadn't she thought of this? So Mona turned away to keep from messing up.

"Well, why are you in trouble," Frank pressed on, not wholly satisfied by the long-winded tale. "If they're Phyllis and Joe's cameras, what does that have to do with you?"

Double Dare

"I'm the dealer," she shot back. "Dealer goes down too," she said like a pro.

Frank didn't know what to say, so he let precious seconds slip between her lie and the incredulity of trying to piece together his thoughts.

"Phyllis already bought Joe's ticket," Mona inserted in the silence. "Which I thought you might like to fly out with him so that you won't feel left out."

"Mo—we don't have—"

"—I already got your ticket. You've got the window seat…in first class," she added for the extra windfall of encouragement.

"That was good Mo! You really worked that one," Phyllis grinned, dancing like a child waiting to see Santa. She plopped down on a lounge chair and kicked her feet up to cross them in front of her, as Mona did the same, plopping in the lounge chair beside hers.

"We've got a long day ahead of us tomorrow," Mona said, full as a tick and happy as a lark. " So, we can't drop the ball this time. We've got to be in full costume when we walk in that courtroom."

Chapter 35

Frank called Joe and they both met up at the airport. Frank and his overnight bag, and Joe and his arsenal.

"Man, you kind of have a lot of baggage there. How long are you planning on staying?" Mona told him it was just an overnight deal, but maybe Phyllis told him something different. Or perhaps after he straightened out this camera fiasco, they were taking that fancy trip to Spain he bragged so much about.

"Yeah man," Joe started, hiking his lips about to head towards that all too familiar bragging territory. "I brought my arsenal those cats out there in Hollywood don't know nothing about."

"Well, check-in is behind you. Better get checked-in before we go through the checkpoint," Frank said.

"I'm already checked-in," Joe said, though oddly standing a ways back from moving towards the check-in line where people were removing their shoes and dropping their carry-on bags into plastic tubs. And this oddness was saying nothing of Joe's festoon look—large meadowlark shades like the kind Lennon and them used to wear in the late 60's, popcorn short pants-set fit for a day on the beach, and bulky Velcro sandals exposing toes not only not manicured, but didn't even look washed, let alone lotioned.

And that was the passable part. The straw fedora cocked to the side of his head with the ten-inch feather hanging over the brim as he chewed a toothpick open like a well-used broom, said something wasn't right.

"You mean you have more bags," Frank asked in awe. "Like man, I know Mona and Phyl said they're raking in doe hand over foot, but I'm sure they didn't hire us our own private jet."

"All man, it's only a few pieces," Joe said, nervously going into explaining what was inside each 50-pound suitcase piled so high on a cart that it looked like he was standing in front of a roll-away dressing room.

"A few? You mean the ticket agents didn't explain anything about the carry-on restrictions?" Frank said shaking his head. "They're—"

"—All man, come on now. Don't go getting like Phyl on me. I'm nerv—not paying $115 a damn bag!"

Frank scanned the cart. It had to be $700 towering over him. "Man, when's the last time you've flown?"

"Plenty of times! Plenty of times," Joe said, trying to find his vain voice, but came up short clinging to his trusty scary voice.

Frank stood there inspecting him, sort of waiting for him to finish. Joe may have thought he had him fooled, talking about the arsenal he packed to show off to Hollywood producers who didn't know anything about his high-tech cameras, but Frank knew good and well no well-traveled man ever carried that many bags on a spur of the moment trip.

"Okay...so it was before 911," he admitted, "but I have flown before," and he turned around trying to see who might be listening, but taking an extra long look at the exit.

"All man, come on and let's get these bags checked before we miss our flight," Frank said, starting to push the cart towards the check-in counter.

"No, hold up man. They want over $1000!" Joe said, grabbing his arm, eyes bulging through the murky meadowlarks. "I don't have that kind of cash on me."

"I'll put it on my credit card. Pay me later," Frank said moving on to the counter.

"Mr. Witherspoon has already checked fourteen bags," said an incredulous check-in agent. "We made an exception as a courtesy to I-Technocon, but we can't check any more bags under his name."

"Well, how about checking them under my name?" Frank pleaded. They had less than thirty minutes to get through security and to the gate.

"Do you work for I-Technocon?"

After some Frank smoozing the agent checked the remaining bags, but only because the plane was half empty, though they still charged that whopping one-grand fee. But at least the gratuity came with a little homemade exclusive humor. The agent shared why the plane was so empty.

"Rarely were planes empty anymore," she laughed, "especially not those flying 3000-miles cross-coast. But then this journalist..." came the punch line, "mistakenly

Double Dare

reported a suspected terrorist flying with 21 bags—and it freed up 300 seats."

Ha. Ha. Ha. Joe hardly laughed. He glared at the ticket agent through the dusky meadowlarks as if he had every intention, and right, to pull the plug on her asinine joke by pulling the cable to the keyboard she typed on.

"How funny was that," Joe scoffed as he fumbled to pull the Velcro on his sandals, hopping around on one foot as he fumbled. "That's what I hate about people like that! She's not even flying but finds it funny to shake people up who are!"

They made it through security and to the gate just as the last person was being checked on the plane.

"Hold up man, I think I forgot some—"

"—Come on Joe! We don't have time. They're about to close the door!"

Turned out there weren't a lot of people flying on this flight, almost as paradoxical to Joe's real reason for his fear of flying. Here they had the first class cabin nearly entirely to themselves, save for the crew who joined them, celebrating a rarity that only happened twice in one flight attendants twenty years of flying, yet Joe coward down in the large leathery seat shaking like a shivering wet leaf. When a flight attendant asked if there was anything he'd like to drink, Frank thought he was going to ask the woman to hold him.

"What the hell is wrong with you," Frank asked, still not wholly clear about why Joe couldn't at least fix the meadowlarks to sit straight on his face ...though he had a pretty good idea.

"Sssh...maannn," he quivered, man-handling both armrests. "I'vve nevvver flown before," he got out at the expense of drawing a small audience taking their first break in years from work. The flight attendants never had so much fun on a flight, or laughed as hard—all 4-hours and 36-minutes they were in the air.

"Mr. Witherspoon, you might want to hold on tight to your seat...we're about to hit a bump," teased one attendant.

Bomp! The plane bounced over an air pocket and Joe cried, "awl maannn, what in the hell is he doing," clutching the armrests so tight his fingers were making permanent indents in the leather.

"You mean she," teased another attendant. "That's why we're flying so light today. She's in training."

"Oh Lawd have mercy, Phyl done set me up. I'ma kill her when I see her. I swear I'ma kill her if I ever get off this thing. I knew there was a reason behind her upping our insurance plans. I should have never signed them papers," he senselessly cried, rocking his head and twisting his body in agony, writhing in the seat.

Now both the meadowlarks and the fedora looked like they were dangling off a coatrack. By the time the plane landed, an imprint of Joe was permanently etched in the seat. Frank looked back and thought he saw his ghost sitting there.

But Joe was so relieved to be on concrete that he ran straight by baggage claim, hand waving in the air all ready to hail a cab.

"You've got to speak the right language with these cabbies…or else they'll take you man," he turned to enlighten Frank, as if 4-hours and 36-minutes hadn't just happened.

"Man, aren't you forgetting something?"

"No, what?" And he really had forgotten.

"Your bags, man!"

Chapter 36

While Frank and Joe were busy getting 21 bags and themselves to the hotel, Mona and Phyllis, and their acting buddies were in rare form, deep in character knocking off the last day of filming, slated to be the longest day of the project.

The courtroom was packed. Lighters, gaffers, fill-ins, editors, spectators, a jury selected out of nowhere, the judge, them, and just anyone outside of this sec who appreciated either courtroom drama, or onstage theatre performances were packed in tight.

Ironically, a flight attendant was on the stand. This was the flight attendant responsible for putting an inept mother and her bawling baby in first class. The two words didn't even belong in the same sentence, but yet there the flight attendant was, well dressed in flying embellishments—white sailor suit decorated with medals from hip to neck displaying her seniority, yet under oath embellishing her tall tail off.

"This was the worst flight I've ever flown," she was saying, shaking her head as if she was in the air when Japanese bombers were trying to get unfriendlies out of their airspace.

"Next! Next!" Jimmy shouted out. "She's the worst liar in all man-made creation! Look at her! She doesn't even realize she's at the wrong trial."

The courtroom erupted in laughter. It was a little funny. The embroidery she wore would elicit that type of laughter. Forget the navy seal pins she decorated herself in, wearing all the white in the world don't make a sailor. She looked like a nurse who knew more about swearing and lying under oath than she knew about medicine.

"Sorry Naomi Campbell…wrong trial! This ain't Pearl Harbor honey!"

More laughter, and one brave spectator who rose from his seat to shout, "All come on your honor, remove that bum from the courtroom!"

But Jimmy sprang out of his seat before the judge could speak and shouted louder. "You idiot," he said pointing at the brave spectator, "you are too fat to talk! So chew on your blubbery lip before I put you on a diet."

The idiot sat down as two courtroom bouncers bounced over to whisper in his ear.

"I bet that really hurt his feelings," Jimmy leaned over and whispered to Mona while the bouncers were chatting with the idiot. "I bet he'll probably think twice before he opens that pie-hole again."

The idiot apparently didn't appreciate what the bouncers had to say, so they had to escort him out of court, yanking him up beneath the armpits as he cried on the way out, "I hope they hang you," he yelled at Jimmy, his voice trailing behind and echoing from the hallway. "I hope they sit your ass in an electric chair and forget to strap you in!"

"Wow, he was really mad," Jimmy leaned over and whispered to Mona again.

"Hear ye, hear ya'll," said the judge. "One more outburst and you will be removed from this trial."

Promptly Jimmy stood up and shouted. "Judge Henry the 4th looks like King Tyrone the 24th today, hear ye' hear yae'! Now, if ya'll all don't mind and excuse the court, I will go on and remove my own self from this trial," he calmly said, pushing in his chair, about to step around Phyllis.

"Not you!" bellowed the judge. "Sit down," he ordered, as the courtroom bouncers met Jimmy at the table.

Jimmy threw out his hands. "But Henry, I mean Tyrone, you just said one more outburst and that person would be excused. Well, I outbursted, and so why am I being discriminated against and not being excused?"

The taking of Naomi's testimony continued, moving in a soft pace tragically designed to run the trial into overtime. It was a given Mona and Jimmy theorized, except they didn't surmise how the thieves could've had editors working congruent to the show Jimmy was putting on to help to liven up their footage. Jimmy caught one editor off to the side splicing while he performed, which made him nervous. They could run his performance right smack dab into the deadline where they'd have no time to edit themselves.

"Hey psst," Jimmy hissed across the table at Mabel who sat on the opposite end…beside Bobby.

Mabel though ignored him, as she had ignored all of them, and that wasn't just all of them seated at the table either, but all of them in the courtroom. She sat at the table as if she was the nicest lady in church sitting on a park bench waiting for the H bus.

"Hey Mabel… peach-a-cobbler lady," Jimmy teased, laughing as he licked his tongue in and out of his mouth. "Your client has a question," he dragged out, ignoring Naomi droning on about the vile, shameful language used on her flight. "Don't make me get up out of my seat and come down there to pinch the part of your hiney hanging off the back of the chair."

He saw her eyes flinch, and dart raggedly in his direction. She still wouldn't acknowledge him though. She was hoping he didn't do anything that stupid. Unfortunately she was hoping against the minion of elitism.

Jimmy hopped up again, telling the judge, and the packed court to put a sock in the yak's mouth for a minute. "I need to confer with our counsel."

"Sit down now!" yelled the judge. Apparently, by the wave of grunts backstroking across the courtroom, Naomi must've been just getting to the juicy part, the part where Jaw recognized he had him three present day kidnappers.

"No!" Jimmy yelled back. "I will not! We have not conferred with our counsel since this parody began. In fact, we have not even been read our rights, so the least you adolescents can do is allow us five minutes to confer with the lovely Marvalette sitting over here."

"All right," Judge Arthur agreed. And why not? It wasn't like they would lose anything by entertaining a short recess.

Mona, Phyllis, Bobby and Jimmy rushed off leaving Mabel at the table. No one seemed to notice, or rather no one cared. The break allowed them to stand around admiring each other's hair and perishable costumes they wore to court that day.

"Do you see what's happening," Jimmy gushed as they rushed for the hallway. Bobby nodded he did. But Mona and Phyllis, not knowing much about film, were clueless.

"I'm going to have to get more drastic in there," Jimmy said, looking into each of their eyes assuring them what he was about to do, and say, wouldn't be viewable for the faint at heart.

Phyllis started to speak, "but—"

—but she was interrupted. "We can't discuss it anymore," and Jimmy cut his eye off to the left where Jaw suddenly stood. "It's done," Jimmy whispered. "The goose is cooked."

Phyllis still didn't understand the code talk, though Mona thought she did, and Bobby definitely did.

Five minutes up and back in the courtroom, Mabel was still seated at the table and another decorated utensil had taken to the witness box.

"For the love of Mother Jezebel, who is this your anus now spilling feces out into the open air," Jimmy started right away, before even taking a seat.

Double Dare

Judge Arthur ignored Jimmy, as did everyone else now used to his outbursts. The pilot flying the day they were escorted off the flight was on the stand.

"The plane literally was shaking, they were keeping up such a commotion back there," the pilot said. "I barely could regain control of the controls. Nearly 300 lives were almost lost that afternoon," he said, letting his head drop to announce the gravity of what almost happened.

"Hey ass wipe," Jimmy slurred. "You know why your plane almost crashed you turd? Because you were in the cockpit jerking off you dick-shit. Clean some of that shit off your windshield and maybe you might be able to see!"

AAAaaaggh! The deep moans and groans waved around the courtroom. "That's enough!," one faint at heart quipped, ahead of another fainter who quipped just a little louder. "Please judge, get him out of here!"

Chapter 37

But Judge Arthur wasn't ready to put Jimmy out just yet. For as repulsive as he was, they wanted to hang on to him for as long as they could, which meant Jimmy had to go for gold.

But before Jimmy got to go for gold, and while the picture was filling in for Mona, two male subjects were making their presence known to anyone with normal hearing in their general vicinity.

"Man, stand over there by that plant," Joe excitedly danced, back in his dry clothes, suited up with three cameras draped around his neck and having traded the meadowlarks for something a little more trendy, and not so remindful of that dreadful trip where he cried the entire way.

Wasn't an exciting plant, and it wasn't even real, just a common shrub that could be found anywhere, though Frank appeased Joe since it was his first time in California as well, and let him snap the picture.

"Oh, Look! I think it's Morgan Freeman coming this way man!"

Frank spun around. He loved Morgan Freeman. He played in all of his favorite movies, none he could call offhand, not that it mattered since he secretly hoped he would run into anyone famous.

"Oh, that dude ain't Morgan," Joe muttered. "Come on, let's get out of this stuffy hotel and go meet us some famous people," Joe cheered on the end. "Man! I'm gonna be talkin' about this trip a long time!"

And Frank knew he would too. It would be 3034 and Joe would be speaking from the grave about the one, and likely only trip, he'd taken to Hollywood. But the story was going to be one of them legends, the kind that every time it was told, a new version would be added. It would go from deciding to fly out with his friend, to receiving a call from Steven Spielberg to help him put the finishing touches on whatever project that would be Spielberg's latest and greatest work. Mention of what really brought them to California, and how he actually arrived would never survive the soaring tales lopped on as the stories advanced.

First thing they noticed...well wait...the first thing Frank noticed after Joe asked 'how he looked' and saw a man dressed in a zoot suit with the fins, were the jazzy vehicles pulling up to the door; nothing later than 2010, or lesser in value than 60-grand.

"Oh shit man," Joe muttered, covering his mouth so one would see what he was thinking.

He was thinking back to pulling up in the Chubby Checker cab with them 21 pieces of his luggage stuffed in the trunk and back seat, with that one large piece bungee-tied to the hood. They must've looked like Fred G. Sanford pulling in. Well guess what? It's not how he was going out.

Joe didn't roll like that. The home he bought should have told everyone that. He turned right around and marched straight up to the concierge and ordered a stretch limo.

"And please," he added, "my wife is down there at the courthouse doing a film, so no hoopty-stretches."

"Oool," the concierge lifted up, "your wife is in that film?" Her eyes fluttered. "Everyone is talking about it. Can you believe some kids would go to that extent just to get attention so that their film would win the fest? ...I mean really? Kidnap a woman? People now-a-days will do anything for 15-minutes of fame."

Frank stiffened. Mona mentioned they were in trouble... but kidnapping? He hoped they hadn't been kidnapped...geez.

But Joe having heard nothing of the sorts was sure the concierge was speaking of another film. "No, my wife is on set, (the only film jargon he knew), with some really serious film people. None of that ruddy-poot stuff for hobbyist," he said.

"Oooh," the concierge obliged him with, deciding this was another elitist with an ego bigger than the script called for.

"Yeah...so don't have us rolling up to the court in no strange-mobile," he said, chuckling proudly. "We want the best."

"Man, how are we going to pay for the best," Frank whispered as they headed for the exit.

"Sssh man! We don't want everyone hearing how short we are," Joe said looking around. "We're playin' with the majors' dude. This is big-time show biz. Let's not mess this up."

A white Rolls Royce, 2011 edition, pulled up to the curb. Joe smiled wide, and even wider when the driver swore the Jackson's sat in his limo all the time. Frank however shrank climbing into the car, and shrank even lower when the driver asked for payment.

Chapter 38

While Frank and Joe paced around a white stretch limo outside the courthouse piecing together a tip for one furious Rolls Royce driver, the big Jaw was making his way to the stand.

"Amber Alert. Amber Alert," Jimmy mocked using his hands like a bullhorn. "Grab your children. Hold their hands…kiss them…this could be the last time you see one of them innocent again."

"Do you swear to tell the truth, the whole truth and nothing but the whole truth," the bailiff asked.

"Hell no!" Jimmy spoke right up. "What the hell is the matter with you bunch of drunkards. Oops, my bad, I forgot where we were, land of the la-la's. You won't know a creep until he has you like this," and he jumped up from the table and dramatically fell over the top, bouncing his nonexistent behind in the air.

The three of them, and quite a few others burst out laughing. Even Mabel looked over and smirked at his behind up in the air trying to quiver, which Mona and Bobby, to the contrary, were supposed to appear in distress…anxiously checking the time, and sweating a little. But Jimmy was good, acting so off the mark bizarre that they couldn't help but laugh too.

"Alright young man, that's enough," said the judge, turning around about to face Jawoski who had taken a seat. He had just put down the gavel down when Jimmy left his position on the table to take to the center of the courtroom.

"I refuse to keep silent about this anymore. Next month I'll be coming out with my memoir about this situation," and he gestured as if he was giving a typical class presentation about butterflies…putting no real extra flair to his voice either.

"But for now," he continued on, raising his voice just a notch. "I'm going to give you all an up close preview of what the most dangerous bully in American dramatic theatre looks like."

He did a Prince move, letting his head drop to alert his viewers that a purple prose was on its way. He jerked up and snapped, "this man here," and he rushed to the stand, legs moving like the Sandman at the Apollo, only faster and spread further apart, to touch the tip of Jawoski's nose with his index finger, though Jawoski did bat his finger away, "pestered me!"

Back to the center of the courtroom, zipping fantastically comical, he put on the rest of his show, crooning, almost to the top of lungs as he sung every third or fourth child's psalm. "He's a child-pesterer I tell you. A repeat offender too. He pestered me over and over and over and over…" crouching lower to the floor each time he said 'and over'. By the time he was on his knees shouting with his hands reaching for the ceiling, "It was horrible…it was horrible…oh God it was horrible," the bouncers were there to finally scrape him off the floor.

"All right...that's enough buddy. You've worn out your stay with us. Be gone!" and they flung him out onto the streets where, of all calamities, he bumped into Joe and Frank still arguing with the limo driver.

"What the hell," Joe mouthed, seeing Jimmy come flying out of the courthouse like a circus clown thrown out of a Ringling Brothers and Barnum & Bailey act.

Jimmy tripped over his foot and toppled down the steps, landing face up to see three strangers, one who upside down looked a lot like Batman.

"Ugh...would one of you gentlemen be so courteous as to give me a lift up?"

Frank quickly extended his hand. "Are you alright fella?"

"Yes," Jimmy replied, brushing himself off as he pulled up to a wobbly stand.

"I don't think they like the way I'm dressed. Bunch of weirdoes and child pesterers in there," he said, about to race off to the hotel.

"Say dude," he chuckled, spinning around as he skipped backwards. "You might want to try standing behind him," pointing to Frank, "because that coyote on your back is going to get tossed out of there too," he laughed before turning around and taking off.

Frank looked at Joe, apologetically as he struggled to hide a small smirk. "Hey—" he started to speak, to Joe's raised palm.

"—Man, don't say nothing to me! Didn't I ask you before we left how I looked?"

"I wasn't going to say anything to you..." Frank stressed on the 'to you' part, that time unapologetically laughing. "I was about to tell the driver to put it all on my credit card," he said, watching Joe's color change from a dark chocolate brown to the rusty hue reflected in those meadowlarks he traded for more trend.

Chapter 39

The thing was, every time the courtroom door opened, or closed, it made this creaking sound. Phyllis, and Mona too, had gotten in the habit of looking back each time they heard the creak...looking for Frank and Joe who'd been sending text messages, on the hour almost, advising them of their whereabouts.

12:09PST (Frank) ...just landed.

1:39PST (Frank) ...in cab... finally!

2:22PST (Joe) ...Phyl—we made it! The plane ride was a little shaky...they had some new broad flying... plus the airline has a lame baggage policy...but we're at the hotel...real lux...and a lot nicer too. See you soon...

And so, ever since those texts the both of them had been inspecting each cranky creak, waiting to hear the creak that would belong to their husbands. For better or worse, despite the small amount Mona explained to Frank, it wasn't going to be enough. She didn't even know exactly what was happening, which to lay out the script with them, during the heat of the moment, could prove disastrous. And poor Phyllis was in even worse shape. Joe, as liberal as he was about things, wasn't nearly as understanding as Frank, who actually was the more conservative. So they sat there at the table, looking back each time the door creaked.

4:04PST the door creaked again. Jaw was still on the stand explaining how he learned Wilma had been kidnapped. In his 32-years of law enforcement, he said he never experienced anything like it.

"She was genuinely afraid for her life," he said just as the door creaked.

"Yeah, we'll see about that," Bobby muttered loud enough for Jaw to hear, though his reaction he missed following Mona and Phyllis's lead, turning around too to see who made the door creak that time.

Confusion ensued as Mona and Phyllis flew to the door to greet Frank and Joe...Joe waving at cameras flickering and flashing...thinking it was all about him.

"Order! Order!" shouted Judge Arthur.

The courtroom bouncers scurried to their feet, rushing up to Mona and Phyllis, only to stop in their tracks as they looked around for direction. But none was to be given because Judge Arthur was embroiled in a heavy discussion with Jaw.

"Hun, try to stay quiet...it's just a mock trial," Mona quickly blurted, for Joe's benefit as well, as they led them up front to the table where Bobby sat intently watching the bitter brawl between the judge and Jaw.

"What's happening," Mona asked Bobby, as Frank and Joe eased into chairs beside them, one vacated by Jimmy, the other by Mabel.

"They're figuring this thing out...about to bring out their star witness," Bobby muttered between his teeth. "Come on Judge Tutt...what's the hold up," he leered. "Bring on the frightened rabbit so we can all move on."

This was the scrambled part of the script, where they were to get the film thieves to think they were watching the clock, still hoping to enter the contest.

Phyllis darted a sharp eye at Mona. Oh God! Joe was going to come out of his skin when, and if the star witness turned out to be Wilma! She'd forgotten about that woman…for some reason seeing her as out of sight, out of mind. The plan they pulled together had her convinced. No one could prove they kidnapped the woman. They had irrefutable proof it didn't happen.

She spun around… "hey hun, me and Mo have been at this mock trial all morning…can you guys run out and bring us back a cup of coffee?"

"Awl Phyl—I left my wallet in the hotel," Joe, flat busted, said as the courtroom erupted into a frenzy.

"What in the hell is this…" Frank mouthed aloud, looking around. The room was packed. Cameras were everywhere, though no celebs he could see were anywhere, while people chanted…'bring her out, bring out your star witness!' And the judge yelled back, 'order in the court!' Phyllis wanted coffee. Mona looked clumsily strange. And like the young kid who tumbled down the steps, he couldn't figure who this other kid was either. Chaos abound.

Phyllis grabbed Mona's hand and shook it. "Let's pray," she said, suddenly remembering to grab Bobby's hand too. "Dear Lord, our Father who art in Heav—"

"—Phyl, what is going on here!?" Joe butted in…

…just as the door creaked yet again.

Chapter 40

Phyllis buckled, but Joe caught her. The creaky door meaning nothing to him distracted him from seeing Wilma enter the courtroom. Bobby and Mona however, and Frank too, saw her enter. Only Frank didn't know Wilma from a cup of molasses dressed how she was. Hearing the chants he only had left to assume he, very likely, was just in time to catch the premier part of the entire mock trial.

"Come on Phyl—shake out of it," Joe was saying, fanning a groggy body hanging limp over the seat.

"Hey man—" Joe said turning to Frank, just about to ask him for spare change so he could buy Phyllis that cup of coffee. But the woman taking the stand caught his attention. From behind she looked familiar. At least that swaggering walk looked like the sway of a woman's behind that had been irking him nearly every damn day for a full ugly year. But he wasn't sure until she turned around and raised her right hand.

Joe slowly removed the goggles as Phyllis fell over the table, spread across it like a ragdoll. "What the—"

"Do you swear to tell the truth, the whole truth, and nothing but the whole truth," the bailiff enunciated in a voice that said he was tired of repeating the same phrase over and over.

"Wilma?" Joe asked peering disbelievingly through the jewels and face painted on a woman who seemed next to impossible to increase in looks. This couldn't be that person. Who would be so cruel to put two of those same women on this world?

"Wilma girl…Waldo is looking for you…" Joe said moving dramatically slow to the center of the court.

But Wilma acted as if Joe was a ghost in the room and she hadn't heard a word. She turned her head to face Judge Arthur as he banged the gavel demanding more order in the court.

"Who is this person!?!" the judge pleaded, straining to find his accomplices, one being the thief among thieves, the elusive Marty himself.

But he found no one because no one but Joe came forward. By this time his accomplices figured out what was happening, or at least a part of what was going on. Not even Mona and Phyllis expected what came next.

"Order! Order!" Judge Arthur cried, so confused he didn't realize that there no longer was any disorder. Spectators sat in the courtroom silent as a funeral, waiting for Joe, holding center court, to perform.

And Joe must have seen his moment too, because he went right into character.

Nodding his head and looking around, he abruptly faced Judge Arthur. "Excuse me your honor, but what in the devil kind of court is this? Don't there usually be some kind of jury box in court? And where's my wife's lawyers? I ain't no lawyer…hu…hu…hu," him laughing, flamboyantly holding his chest flashing three gaudy rings in a row.

Double Dare

"That's right," a spectator spoke up. "We want to vote on this trial!"

"Oh God," Phyllis muttered, dragging her head up off the table to get a peek at Joe's performance.

"But the star witnesses' hasn't yet testified," Bobby shouted, springing out of his seat.

"Shut up," Phyllis said, nudging Bobby. "We don't need her to speak!"

"Oh, yes we do," Bobby excitedly said, ignoring her nudging and pulling on the hem of his jacket, as a loud cry for jurors erupted through the court.

"Hold up! Hold up!" Joe hollered over the rising tempo calling for jurors.

"Wait," Joe hissed, unable to stop the cries. "Give me this," and he snatched the gavel off the judge's desk, banging it against the side paneling of wood closet to him.

"Shut up!" he shouted. "Before I come out there and start knocking this thing against some heads."

The noise piped down and again everyone waited, Mona and Phyllis especially.

"Oh God..." Phyllis moaned, in hymnal with Mona. "I hope he doesn't blow it..."

"I hope this little skit was a lot of fun and you enjoyed yourself," he said to Wilma, who still refused to look at him. "But then I knew they shouldn't have hired you no way," he grumbled, rolling his eyes and turning around to face his waiting audience.

"My name is Joe Carenthesis Witherspoon," he said as Phyllis muttered another one of her 'Oh God's,' and sliding one hand over her face.

"And that over there is my lovely wife of 21-years, Mrs. Phyllis Ann Witherspoon," he said.

"Mo—please call me an ambulance," Phyllis said, sliding down more in her chair. "No! Better yet, just go on and call me a hearse."

"—And what I'm here for," Joe continued on, "I'm looking for the fella, or fellas, that's crying about how they need help with them fifty ISP cameras my wife sold that they don't understand—"

"—cause there won't be no refunds…oh no…and double that hell no! I-Techno don't do no refunds!"

Epilogue

What happened?

Wilma left the stand and shook Bobby, Phyllis, and especially energetically, Mona's hand, thanking them profusely for pulling together the best parody she had ever personally experienced. Tears were in her eyes as she spoke, though they quickly dried up when she looked over at Joe. And even still, she went on to find investors to rebuild and reopen Hobb Knobb.

'Long live the arts, where her heart and soul would forever remain,' she cried.

Mona had done her homework…as usual. The flyer Wilma picked up off her car was a contract asking for her participation to play the leading role in the film project...Double Dare...which commenced when she arrived at the theatre.

No one, except for the writers/directors Mona and Bobby, knew the full script despite, as the parody began playing out, finding themselves many times having to ad hoc things.

So, a hand clap and standing ovation to them all for inventing an outrageous parody that brought together truth and dare and consequences all in the name of fun and entertainment. There was no film thief, but rather a loosely scripted script that kept everyone, including the main cast...Wilma, Mona, Phyllis, Jimmy, Bobby, and even Judge Arthur...alias Marty, guessing.

Double Dare came in first place at the film festival. They received that $75,000 purse, and movie option, which Joe quickly helped himself to the purse, though just for the photo op. That was his opportunity to make sure everyone knew where those high-tech cameras came from...which he, of course, landed two buyers out of that advertisement.

And still, everyone had a blast. The secondary cast; the banker and store manager, they wanted in from the moment Bobby explained what he was doing. He was a good kid. It was the least they could do. But too bad the bank manager had to be edited from the film. Jimmy only could use the scene where he and Bobby jetted out of the bank holding up the moneybags. The other footage, with the manager in it, only showed the three of them in his office laughing and talking about regular stuff; him asking about their grades and how school was coming along, and telling them to be careful before a real robber saw them with all that money.

Overall, it was an experience each of them would fondly remember. Well, all except for the woman on the flight. Unfortunately, she was real. But then she was upgraded to first class. Hopefully it helped ease her discomfort some.

The flight attendant and pilot however, were last minute add-ons, and good sports, as were the agents, thanks to Wilma who was the biggest sport, working entirely without a script.

Film tag line: Desperate dreamers double dare each other to kidnap a local businesswoman to boost attention to win a national film festival contest. The kidnapping, and subsequent melee 'cleverly' becomes their footage.

Moral to the Story: To own your work, you must not only know the material, and believe it, but you must have given birth to it.

Double Dare

LATEST BOOKS

A Blast From the Past, Poetry Collection (2012)

Mindless, Fiction/Mystery (2012)

Lock Box, Fiction/Paranormal Mystery (2012)

ROMANCE SERIES

Leiatra's Rhapsody, a Novel (2008) – Book I

Something Xtra Wild, a Novel (2009) – Book II

This One I Got Right, a Novel (2010) – Book III

Rye and the Rump, a Novel (2011) – Book IV

My Love, Fiction/Contemporary Romance (2012) – Book V

MORE

GEM: A Collection of Poetry, Short Stories, and a One-Act Play (2008)

Black Table, a Memoir/Essays (2009)

Pretty Inside Out, Fiction (2009)

Tehuelche, a Novel (2010)

Storytella, a Short Story Collection (2010)

Pleasure, Fiction/Erotic Romance (2011)

A Piece of Peace, Spiritual Romance Fiction (2011)